SEVEN NOTEBOOKS

ALSO BY CAMPBELL McGRATH

SEVEN NOTEBOOKS

POEMS

CAMPBELL McGRATH

An Imprint of HarperCollins*Publishers*

HarperCollins books may be purchased for educational, business, or sales promotional use. For information, please write: Special Markets Department, HarperCollins Publishers, 10 East 53rd Street, New York, NY 10022.

FIRST EDITION

Designed by Cassandra J. Pappas

Library of Congress Cataloging-in-Publication Data

McGrath, Campbell, 1962–
Seven notebooks : poems / Campbell McGrath. — 1st ed.
p. cm.
ISBN: 978-0-06-125464-2
I. Title
PS3563.C3658S48 2008
811'. 54—dc22
2007030331

08 09 10 11 12   ID/RRD   10 9 8 7 6 5 4 3 2 1

For Elizabeth

ACKNOWLEDGMENTS

With thanks to Florida International University and the John D. and Catherine T. MacArthur Foundation for economic support; to Robert Hass for the translations of Bashō borrowed for "Blueberry Notebook"; and to the editors who published these poems, sometimes under previous titles, in the following magazines, journals, anthologies and websites:

Agni; *The Atlantic Monthly*; *Barrow Street*; *Best American Poetry 2007*; *Cake*; *Call Review*; *Colorado Review*; *Crab Orchard Review*; *Cue*; *Five Points*; *Fugue*; *Indiana Review*; *Kenyon Review*; *Michigan Quarterly Review*; *Mid-American Review*; *MiPOesias*; *New American Writing*; *New England Review*; *The New Yorker*; *Ocho*; *Ontario Review*; *Pleaides*; *Ploughshares*; *Poetry*; *Poetry Daily*; *Poetry Northwest*; *Pool*; *Salmagundi*; *Sentence*; *Slate*; *Sub-Lit*; *Tri-Quarterly*; *Under the Rock Umbrella: Contemporary American Poets* (Mercer University Press, 2006); *Virginia Quarterly Review*.

CONTENTS

CIVILIZATION NOTEBOOK

PAPYRUS NOTEBOOK

DAWN NOTEBOOK

HURRICANE NOTEBOOK

LUXURY NOTEBOOK

ASTRAL NOTEBOOK

BLUEBERRY

NOTEBOOK

ODE TO INSPIRATION

Then the imagination withdraws, drifts across the table
to investigate the glass flowers rolled in cloth tape.

It hovers, probes the petals, some like galaxies,
some like figs or seashells. Dutiful and penitent,

it shimmers back across the gulf of air,
without a metaphor, to doze away the afternoon.

Rain.
Unseasonably hot day.

Imagination is the builder, the worker bee,
but inspiration is the queen.

And when she leaves me, where does she go
if not back to the hive to gorge on royal jelly,

back into her cave of winds, accumulating
density, growing richer and darker,

like mercury in the bloodstream,
like extravagant honey.

Ocean like beaten metal removed from the cooling pail,
mark of the hammer and tongs, the smith's signage,
grain revealed as by pressure of the burin in a Japanese
    print,
substantial, bodily, color of agave, color of bitter medicine,
translucent only when the waves rise up to break at the bar,
fingered by sun to the texture of meringue or Verano glass.
Miami is not famous for its seashells. This beach,
continually eroded, is held together by borrowed sand,
graded by tractors at dawn, willed into place by the
    tourism industry.
But today, after a weeklong barrage of northeast winds,
it resembles the famous shell beds of Sanibel,
though these are mostly bits and pieces arrayed in
    sinuous drifts,
the frilled lips and spooned-out tails of horse and queen
    conchs,
sponge tubes, varieties of seaweed and uprooted coral,
tiny broken elkhorn infants, torn fans, punch cards,
serrated disks and tribal ornaments, teeth, dismembered
    ears
and bleached stone knuckles of a skeleton seeking
    restitution.

And the eye, from its cupola of privilege, scanning the
    wreckage
to seize upon the unbroken cylinder of an olive shell,
paired lightning whelks revolving in the wash,
purple scallop overwritten with calcified worm tunnels—
how does it know to seek out only perfect forms?

Breakfast: two clementines and a blueberry yogurt while reading Neruda on the porch. The students are agitating for me to teach the Whitman & Neruda seminar, a class I have promised and failed to deliver for how many years now? "Ode to Criticism." "Ode to Eel Chowder." Read this week that blueberries have been determined to be a nutritional super food, a mighty antioxidant endowed with mysterious power to supercharge the brain and all but assure eternal life. Yes, but will they cure my aching feet? My policy is to ignore bodily afflictions for at least six months, but my days of running on the beach appear to be at an end. Temporarily, I'd like to believe. I am a good patient, performing all the podiatrically prescribed exercises and therapeutic routines—ice, stretching, a stupid boot I must wear to sleep like an antipodal dunce cap to passively stretch my plantar fascia, the tendonlike bundle of tissue that underlies the arch of the foot and bears upon it the body's weight, anatomical detail of which I have resided in delightful ignorance heretofore. As a rule, you notice the plantar fascia only when it cries out in pain. And then, if you continue to run on it, for weeks, and even months, I suppose you get what you deserve. Swimming is better anyway—I should take a swim in the ocean! But school is in session—there is work to be done! Beautiful morning, sunny and cool, the archway hidden beneath cascading alamanda blossoms the color of Irish butter. No, I do not feel like working, or exercising: I feel like reading poetry. "Ode to Laziness." "Ode to Walt Whitman." Still cannot grasp Neruda to my satisfaction. There is about him something of the conger eel, I believe. And something of the plantar fascia. And something of the blueberry.

ODE TO THE PLANTAR FASCIA

Latin cousin to Achilles,
architectural upholder
bearing its magisterial bundle
beneath an imperial arch,
rods around ax
around
axle and axis,
staunch stanchion of the canonical self,
aquiline and august,
tensile, earthly, planted
and wound in sinewed plaits,

inverted hammock
on which the body rests its burden
like a red-faced tourist
in the shadow
of a coconut palm,

only now is your grievance
made known to me,
only now do I hear your cry,
unenviable membrane,
faithful attendant upon my every stride,
tender sole, antipodal to the soul,

pale mirror to the palm
of this hand,

only now do I honor your service,
and my dignity is hobbled,
only now do I learn to address you by name,

and the Empire
trembles.

Flocks of ibis on old tractors in cleared fields sliding to sawgrass,

cartloads of corn, or mangoes, or clean fill dirt,

orchards of citrus and avocado, shade houses of the enigmatic orchid growers,

dusty horses in a crude corral fashioned from cypress limbs where the canal is edged with sugarcane and banana trees by the freight tracks

hard against the *Casa de Jesus*,

convicts collecting trash along the roadside in their FLA CRIMINAL JUSTICE jumpsuits with the SHERRIF'S DEPT school bus on the shoulder, joyless troopers overseeing what appears to be a collection of high school kids caught with bags of pot in the glove compartments of their Trans Ams,

security towers around the Krome Immigration Detention Center, razor-wire reefs on which the rough boats of the *loas* bound for Lavilokan have run aground, gravel quarry gouging the template, coral rock pits and barrows,

panel truck offering shrimp and stone crab claws from the Keys,

pickups selling roasted corn or watermelons, pickups heading into the fields loaded with campesinos,

faces of the Maya picking pole beans in the Florida sunshine,

Krome Avenue: the Third World starts here.

———

Midwinter, and we have come to pick strawberries and tomatoes, flowers and herbs, our annual nod to hunting and gathering, a voyage into the remnants of agricultural South Florida, vanishing order endangered as the legendary panther. Sure enough, Rainbow Farms has been swallowed by exurbia, and we must head farther south in search of a passable field, crossing the canals where anhinga hitch their wings to hang like swaths of drying fabric beside the dye vats on the rooftops of Marrakech, tree farms and nurseries on all sides, freeholds of the Old

Floridians or *ranchitos* run by cronies of long-deposed cau-
dillos, ranks of potted hibiscus and parti-colored bougain-
villea, bromeliads, queen palms, Hawaiian dwarf ixora.
When we finally find a strawberry field it's late afternoon
and many have given up, but there are still a few families
in the rows, hunched *abuelas* with five-gallon buckets they
will never fill today, and I wander out among them and
lose myself altogether.

The strawberries are not fully ripe—it is the cusp of the
season—yet the field has been picked over;

we have come too early, and too late.

Lush, parsley-green, the plants spread their low stalks to
flower like primitive daisies and I seek the telltale flash of
red as I bend to part the dust-inoculated leaves, spooking
the lazy honeybees, but mostly there is nothing, the ber-
ries are pale, fuzzed nubs. Of the rest what's left are the
morbidly overripe, fly-ridden berries melted into purple
froth and those just at the bursting brink of rot—in the
morning, if you bring them home,

these will wear a blue-green fur, becoming themselves
small farms, enterprising propagators of mold.

But here's one perfect, heart-shaped berry, and half a row later, three more, in the shadows, overlooked. Where has my family gone? Where is everybody? I find myself abandoned in the fields, illumined by shafts of sunlight through lavender clouds, bodiless, unmoored and entirely happy.

White eggplant and yellow peppers—
colored lanterns of the Emperor!

Lobular, chalk-red, weevil-scarred tomatoes—
a dozen errant moons of Neptune!

Vidalia onions seized by their hair and lifted
to free a friendly giantess from the soil!

Snapdragons!
They carry the intonation of Paris

on a rainy day in May, granitic odor of pears,
consensus of slate and watered silk.

Elizabeth snips a dozen stems
with flower shears

scented by stalks of sage,
rosemary, flowering basil, mint.

————

From here the city is everything to the east, endlessly rami-
fied tile-roofed subdivisions of houses and garden apart-
ments, strip malls, highway interchanges, intransigent
farmers holding their patchwork dirt together with melons
and leaf lettuce—the very next field has been harrowed
and scoured and posted for sale—already in our years here
it has come this far, a tidal wave of human habitation, a
monocultural bumper crop. And to the west is the Ever-
glades, reduced and denuded but secure, for the historical
moment, buffered and cosseted, left hand protecting what
the right seeks to destroy. And where they meet: this fer-
tile border zone, contested marginland inhabited by those
seeking refuge from the law or the sprawl or the iron cus-
tody of the market, those who would cross over in search
of freedom, or shelter, or belief, those who would buy into
this world and those who would be rid of it alike in their
admiration and hope for and distrust of what they see.
And what they see is this: Krome Avenue. What they see
is the Historical Moment caged in formidable automobiles
gorging on fast food, definitive commodities of the previ-
ous century to be supplanted by what? The next Historical

14

Moment, and the next, like a plague of locusts descending upon the fields, or the fields descended upon, or these fields, now, just as they are.

———

This may be the end of it, I suspect, the last year we make this effort. The kids are getting older and less pliable, the alligators in the irrigation canals pushed ever farther west, carrying into the heart of the sawgrass the reflection of a world grown monstrous and profound. If so, I will miss the scratched hands and the cucumber vines, ranks of hibiscus focusing their radar on the sun, the taste of stolen strawberries eaten in the rows, chalky and unwashed, no matter their senselessness here, in fields reclaimed from subtropical swamp, these last remaining acres empty or picked over or blossoming or yet to blossom, again fruit, again spoilage, again pollen-heavy dust.

No, the Third World does not begin at Krome Avenue, because there is only one world—.

It's late. Cars are pulling out, mobile homes kicking up gravel, a ringing in my ears as of caravans crossing the Sahara resolves to Elizabeth calling on the cell phone—*hey, where are you?* I can see her by the farm stand, searching the plots and rows, not seeing me, still drifting, afloat, not yet ready to be summoned back. *It's time to go—where have you been?*

Where have I been, can I say for certain?

Where have I been?

But I know where I am—I'm here, in the strawberry field.

Here.

I'm right here.

ODE TO A CAN OF SCHAEFER BEER

We would like to
express sincere
thanks to our
Schaefer customers
for their loyalty
and support.

It is brewed in Milwaukee, Wisconsin.
It knows its place.
It wears its heart on its sleeve
like a poem,
laid out like a poem
with weak line endings and questionable
closure. Its idiom
would not be unfamiliar
to a Soviet film director,
its emblem a stylized stalk
of bronzed wheat,
circlets of flowering hops
as sketched by a W.P.A. draftsman
for a post office mural in 1936.
It conjures a forgotten social contract
between consumers and producers,
a world of feudal fealty—
the corporation

is your friend, your loyalty
shall be rewarded—a vision
of benign paternalism
last seen in *Father Knows Best*
and agitprop depictions of Mao
sharing party wisdom with eager villagers,
bestowing avuncular unction.

It was, once, *the one
beer to have
when having more than one,*
slogan and message
outdated as giant ground sloths roaming
the forests of Nebraska,
irrecoverable
as the ex-cheerleader
watching her toddler eat handfuls of sand
at the playground
considers that lost world of pompoms
and rah-rah-let's-go-team
to be.

It has earned no lasting portion of glory.
It has eaten crow
and humble pie. Long before it was faded

by the sun it appeared
faded by the sun, gathering dust
in the corner
of the bodega or the county store,
cylindrical, handy, holsterable,
its modesty honestly
come by, possessing the courage
of its simple convictions
like the unsuspected gunfighter
emerging from shadow
to defend the weak from tyranny.

And if we have moved forward,
unmasking the designs of the regime
upon our fertile valley,
learning to litigate against the evil sheriff,
such knowledge has left a bitter taste
in our mouths,
and if this can of beer
deserves our attention
it is as a reminder of what it meant
to speak without hypocrisy,
to live unironically,
to be sincere.

Thin, rice-sweet, tasting of metal
and crisp water,
it is no worse than many,
and if it is not an elixir it might serve
as an occasional draft
of refreshment and self-knowledge.

It was established in the United States in 1842.
It contains 12 fl. oz.

Store in a cool place
and drink responsibly.

ODE TO BUREAUCRATS

I cherish tongs
and scissors
—PABLO NERUDA, "Ode to Things"

Practitioners of oblivion, signatories
of arcane regret
without whose seal we may not enter
into paradise appropriately
entailed,
fated duty, the onus
of their diligence,
the layers of it,
sanctified and sacrificial,
rheum
of pallid eyeballs
immured
in fluorescent cubicles,
municipal camouflage
of coffee rings
and uniform collars,
vestibules of onionskin,
reams and sheets
and terminals,
inkless stick pens
chained to gouged linoleum

as if to strike blood from a twig,
their codes and initials and #2 bubbles,
verification and secondary verification,
their official contrition,
their sorrow, for
there is nothing to be done,
the renewal date has passed,
the balance is insufficient,
the identification numbers do not match,
the procedure is not covered,
the check is in the mail,
the scissors you ordered have arrived
in your office
and they are blunt and monstrous
as the bill of a stork
gone mad
in mating season,
scissors an irascible child might have fashioned
from humble elements
as a plaything,
hinged flanges forged
from metal too weak to whet or hone
bloodied by thumbs
razored

on ragged iron finger rings,
low-bid scissors
procured by central purchasing,
scissors only the immortal
Chairman could love,
cheap scissors, bad scissors, apocalyptic scissors,
these are your scissors,
Mr. McGrath,
sign here,
please, front and back,
in triplicate.

2 a.m: looking at photos of Neruda's house in Isla Negra after the troops got through with their vandalism, a bit half-hearted, really, as if even the Generalissimo's thugs were intimidated by the great man, the poet of the people. He loved perfect shells, rare specimens from the Maldives, Tahiti, the South China Sea, nothing like what we find here:

shark's eye worked down to the least inner whorl;

sensual architecture of a lightning whelk, postmodern staircase to and from nowhere;

elongated pearly sweep of a cream-colored conch, its sand-abraded chamber laid bare, apse of a ruined cathedral, view-hole to the wood-grain desk beyond—

the way a poem appears

first as a texture felt and understood by steady pressure of the mind, an alluvial Braille of oceanic gravity,

intuitive shape worn smooth by tidal revision.

The more I read Neruda the more I am drawn to him and the less I understand him as a person and a poet. How to reconcile his loyalty to the sacred memory of Lorca and Valléjo and Hikmet, with the abandonment of his new-born daughter, sickly and foredoomed, barely acknowledging, years later, notice of her death? Against the deep attention and clarity of the *Odes* the erotic conquistador vanity of the *Memoirs*; against his blood-scrawled passion for the Spanish Republic his self-exculpatory defense of Stalin's empire. Traveling the Soviet Union he exalts the grandeur of power lines above the ruined plains of Central Asia, the brotherhood of workers in failed collectives, the defense of freedom in kangaroo courts. *The church I like best is the hydroelectric plant* . . . Even his bodies are wrought of sentimental steel, mythologized to moonglow and honeysuckle blossoms, breasts of the goddess candied and epic, strongmen squeezing eggplants to blood and purple pulp, eager products of the five-year plan. Neruda among the potassium miners and aluminum smelters, the farmers and fishermen, his voters, his readers, his lovers, his constituents, always the masses, always the People, always the gestural sweep of categorical imperatives, hortatory whirlpool in which individual destinies dissolve. The transformative magic of language is precisely its ability to reveal or to deny, to lay bare or dissemble, to unlock our shackles or participate in our enslavement. Against ideology the testimony of the senses;

against the rhetoric of power the reproach of an image.

Stalin: *A single death is a tragedy, a million deaths is a statistic.*

Bashō:

> *Very brief:*
> *gleam of blossoms in the treetops*
> *on a moonless night.*

Coolness of the melons
flecked with mud
in the morning dew.

What is the subject of this poem by Bashō?
Melons, dew, farming, food, human existence
and its inextricable enmeshing with the cycles
of the seasons and of night and day?
What is the subject of Bashō's haiku taken
collectively? The world or the observer,
that which is perceived or the act of perception?
Or the act of depiction? Or, complexly,
their interaction? Or, somehow: *language*?
The medium is both subject and object,
the medium is the message? Is this not akin
to saying that ice skating is all about the ice?
But then, what else is ice skating about—
bodies in motion, escaping winter boredom?
What can it mean to call any image "objective"?
Of what would an utterly egoless art consist
except silence? Does refusing to create negate
the self or condemn it to the gulag of the interior?
Where does the poetry voice go when it goes?
I don't know. I only hope it comes back.

C: Then what sort of consciousness does lyric poetry accommodate?

P: Is it mimetic?

R: Well, if it was "actual" consciousness we'd need to serve our brain up with the poem.

T: Or maybe we project it, re-create that consciousness within the reader, a mode of perceiving—can we situate the consciousness external to the text?

J: Like images—

T: That flashcard thing, the image going off in the reader's head, the lightbulb thing.

J: But images are pretty easy—pretty clear-cut. I mean, there's Molly, I see Molly, you know, sitting there—I see that image.

R: Is Molly an image?

Y: Or is Molly a thing, an entity, an object in the universe?

J: Well, yeah, she is—but I can see her, that's my image.

R: So anything you see is an image?

S: I'm not sure I agree with John. . . .

M: I object to being appropriated like this. . . .

A: Objectified!

T: So, we see Molly, but maybe that's just an ocular image, not an image in a poetic sense.

C: Maybe her purple shirt is an image—"I see Molly in a shirt the color of the flowers we planted that were eaten by the snails." That might be an image. Dahlias.

R: But that's a story—you've attached a narrative to the image. It's not just the purple, it's the snails, things growing and being consumed.

S: That sounds like Bashō!

T: Typical. . . .

A: Can we get back to workshopping now, please?

ODE TO BLUEBERRIES

All the new poems are about blackberries.

But to praise the blueberry
is to praise the ordinary and easily obtained
pleasures of this world,
spartan gems
in green plastic baskets,
summer's common caviar, rank-and-file
pie-fillers, foot soldiers
sprung from hardscrabble soil
bearing bandoliers of edible bullets
from Skowhegan, Maine,
to Abbotsford, British Columbia.
Even in New Jersey,
industrial mother of cities and great poets,
choleric and densely arteried,
even along the tea-colored rivers
east of Camden they thrive,
five-pointed "star berry"
beloved of the indigenous peoples,
native forage of the black bear
and sprightly deer
as numerous now as when the colonizers
first appeared in those

marshy bays and estuaries
lined with cattails and summer homes.

Despite which history
there is no national hymn to the blueberry,
no Whitmaniacal encomium,
no mythos,
no pantheon or canon.
Blueberries inhabit the uncultivated
margins of our imagination,
easily overshadowed
by the succulence of strawberries,
overawed by the patriotic
stature of the apple, the exotic
individualism of coconut and kiwi,
against which they project
the bland,
antiheroic identity
of the collective, entirely pluralistic,
a democracy of spheres,
the sour purple pea-sized berries
and the bitter green
beadlings and the ordinary citizens
in crisp blue tunics

fattening with sugar week by week
as the season swells to perfect ripeness.

And then declines.

Summer passes. Blueberries disappear
unremarked from our midst
as autumn's grasping hand grows skeletal,
and the first snow settles
upon drifted oak and maple leaves.

And if, in their early winter rambles,
they were to happen upon that
brittle, fine-branched, pale-leaved bush,
they might mistake it for
forsythia,
more likely they would not
pay it any mind
at all, those
eager American poets
traveling ever deeper into the forest
in pursuit of the legendary,
labyrinthine,

bramble-tangled temple
of the blackberry.

Tell me, which is it
they have come to adore,
the fruit
or the thorns?

And the weather of paradise continues. Ocean breeze, cool air, hot sun. Three kinds of lizards abounding in the yard, chameleons, geckos and anoles, feeling the pull of denser sunlight, its cyclic power, arc and declination. Yesterday we found their eggs in the leaf mold by the sidewall of the garden. Oh, to be a reptile! Worked hard at the university all week, rode the exercise bike this morning. At least my foot does not hurt. Then shopping for vital supplies—the boys sprout like saplings and shed their clothes as leaves. Then to visit the grandparents at their condo. A nice swim, water clear and green and warmer, fast-moving skies, zinc and teal, light a kind of melted wax or sleet, ocean all sandy froth. At low tide we walk out to the sandbar, shin deep, the boys wrestling and playing, Elizabeth with her parents on the beach. Later I doze off by the pool. Evening now, the lights coming on, candles and lanterns, a white tent on the sand—French people are having a party!

LINCOLN ROAD

Browsing, before dinner, at Books & Books,
checking out the new poems
in the new journals, the vast glass panes thrust against
by shoppers and gawkers on Lincoln Road
emit a particular cautionary hum
as they insist upon delimiting inside from out,
tongued and grimed by the fingerless
gloves of the homeless,
bodies gesturing and melding back
into the pyroclastic flow,
someone considering black lingerie next door,
bedside lamps of Italian design,
something sleek to refresh the kitchen—*honey,
a silver pasta fork?*—
tattooed dance clubbers and waitresses
slaloming trays through the crowd,
a woman selling jewelry knit from optical fibers
lurid as stationary fireworks, pages
of a Carioca newspaper
turning, foil off a champagne bottle golden
against the tile, pink straws, the splash
of modest fountains
in common space, a baby
in green hip harness
staring back at me goggle-eyed, recording it all

like the tourists with digital camcorders
pre-editing their memories
and the ringing of cell phones broadcasting
a panegyric of need
with whichever hooks and trembles
we have chosen in the darkness to answer.

NERUDA

A materialist.
A collector and a collective.
A national museum.

Curator of wordplay and world ego,
luxurious seashells and Guamanian coconut stamps,
bells, figureheads, ships in bottles,
roots and smooth stones.

Nature, but not raw,
nature humanized and ameliorated,
as if he would inhabit it
eye to eye,
erotically coequal to its hand-worked figurations—
driftwood snakes, fruit flies in amber,
horses in a snowy show ring.

Ringmaster,
wielder of the whip.

And, concomitant, essential human forms
and artifacts: carnelian broach,
giant shoe from the village cobbler in Temuco—

but not the vast forests of childhood,
not the cordilleras at dawn.

Not a fact-checker, not a scrupler.

A maestro, an impresario,
president of Pablo Neruda Enterprises,
director of the great public works project: Pablo Neruda.

Always Neruda, never Reyes or Basoalto.
Neruda, Neruda.

Raices y piedras: Neruda.

Rain. Purple dahlias in plastic buckets, sacks of topsoil, a bent trowel. A week later the snails have eaten the dahlias and when we plant coleus in their place we remember to lace the soil with poison pellets. That the world is ultimately unknowable makes images so complexly evocative. Music, sunlight through the slats of the broken window shade, perception, the apprehensible, drawn into the mystery of the senses, fingering the shards of the mosaic, pebbles flecked with tourmaline, their weight, their smoothness in the palm while the fingertips read their facets as beveled ridgelines eroded as the wave-worn striations of a seashell. Texture of our days so hard to pin down: the action figures in the bathtub and the eggshells in the sink and the *Martha Stewart Living* on the floor and the catalogs and the mall and the Jackie Chan movie we took the boys to see and the pizza restaurant where the charming Brazilian waitress brings us, as a special favor, glasses of the frozen after-dinner drink we secretly detest. Stop. Or, slow down. Hours pass, a night, a week of sickly dawns. Light doubly filtered through the palm fronds and white lace curtains to the wooden floor scored by old termite tunnels, termite colonies rising and falling, empires chained to iron wheels and slick metal cogways, pistons, belts, engines idling in vast machine sheds as the night crew emerge from their labor into fog from the ice-bound Monongahela. Snow exists only on the tarpaper roofs and the slick skins of the automobiles, quickly melted as the steam rises from their coffee and the smokestacks imply the arrow of human intention by their strict verticality against the sky's infinite and infinitely erasable vision field. Liminal. Ice on a river, forming, a journey taken, the flow, ice melting back into the stream bearing the marks of the ice skaters on its hide, its rind, runes of elaborate randomness chiseled in frozen dust. Life in the surface of things, artifactual energy, layer upon layer, room after room, paper through the printing press overwritten with inscrutable directions, sheets cut and bound, and handled, and sold, and shelved in the great library of time, and lost, and rediscovered, and shredded to be thrown as confetti at the ticker-tape parade of a forgotten hero. Winter birds. Weeds poking up at the edge of the asphalt. Shoes piled in a basket by the door. Umbrellas, a lunchbox, a brown paper shopping bag, the familiar loops of its handles, arc of the string like the curve of the skater's trajectory and the steam from the cooling towers blown west. Or south. Deep familiarity of the house. A green candle, photographs in silver frames, impression of a canceled stamp. And in the morning Elizabeth calls us to the garden to see what our husbandry has wrought: a massacre of snails.

CIVILIZATION

NOTEBOOK

TIME

Not an absence but a presence,
dense as any mineral, certain as sour wood.

We move through it like termites
tunneling dim passages beneath the visible,

miners seeking a way forward with faulty lamps,
brief lights in the blackness, the match-strike

of consciousness enacting its doomed insurgency
against the dark mountain.

•

What has made it impossible for us to live in time like fish in water, like birds in air, like children? It is the fault of Empire! Empire has created the time of history. Empire has located its existence not in the smooth recurrent spinning time of the cycle of the seasons but in the jagged time of rise and fall, of beginning and end, of catastrophe. Empire dooms itself to live in history and plot against history. One thought alone preoccupies the submerged mind of Empire: how not to end, how not to die, how to prolong its era.

—J. M. COETZEE, *Waiting for the Barbarians*

•

In Flight, Chicago to Miami

Never seen Lake Michigan frozen solid this far out, and from the commuter plane the smaller ponds in Michigan, with the pitched huts of ice fishermen, sometimes a pickup truck out on the ice, small dark circles carved in the frozen skin of the water. Which way do those portals open? What form of transit, what commerce between the realms? Black trees, white snow, bare fields, farms, industrial zones, open lots bereft of significance, hotels, taverns. Now the city—most of its energy in roads, redundant avenues of connection. Or, contradictorily, in walls: the endless blocks of bungalows lined up on the West Side, narrow snow-covered strips of earth between them, walled and apart, neighbor from neighbor—how much more logical to build a giant hive, to live in a hive, unity of the hive-mind—

————

Sound asleep for forty minutes, music playing unheeded in my ears. Waking up I check the iPod and can precisely time, by the last song I remember hearing, how long I was gone. But where did I go? Then to the window: just the pattern I was looking for,

titanic imbroglio of gerrymandered fields,

dark woods in the organic vertiginous ridges and hollows, not fiery enough for a Van Gogh, more proto-geometrical, like Klimt in a palette borrowed from Georgia O'Keeffe.

Passing over Tallahassee now, up ahead I can glimpse the Gulf—we will strike it near the Big Bend, land of dead raccoons on two-lane roads leading through cedar swamps to lonely fishing outposts. Lumber companies own most of this, biding their time, waiting for the next few million sun-seekers to pave and deflower it. What does this wilderness contain that could pose any risk to the Empire? Black bears, poisonous snakes? Where are the barbarians?

Where are the barbarians now that we need them?

Looking for Cedar Key—have we passed it? Low clouds far below, shadows offset on the pale green Gulf like a print effect, more Hokusai than Hiroshige. Now subdivisions abutting the last swamp forests, the northern extremities of Tampa, golf courses and marinas, wildfires of some sort in distant scrubland, salt water merging with the land, emerging from the silk of its eminence to crawl, bellywise, into the undergrowth, and burrow into the sandy soil, and wait. What shall be born of that union—

creature with seashell ears and vines for hair,
mermaids fed on manatee milk?

Florida, glorious and venal as the emerald-crusted scepter
of a potentate long vanished beneath the waves,
flush, gilded, not the lilies
but the light itself—well, yes, the lilies, too,
and all the nameless shaken blossoms of this state.

•

To critique historicism in all its varieties is to un-learn to think of history as a developmental process in which that which is possible becomes actual by tending to a future that is singular. Or, to put it differently, it is to learn to think of the present—the "now" that we inhabit as we speak—as irreducibly not-one.

The futures that "are" are plural, do not lend themselves to being represented by a totalizing principle, and are not even always amenable to the objectifying procedures of history writing. For my "I am as having been" includes pasts that exist in ways that I cannot see or figure out—or can do so sometimes only retrospectively. Pasts *are* there in taste, in practices of embodiment, in the cultural training the senses have received over generations. They are there in practices I sometimes do not even know I engage in. This is how the archaic comes into the modern, not as a remnant of another time but as something constitutive of the present.

—DIPESH CHAKRABARTY, *Provincializing Europe*

•

NOW

The future does not exist.

It is a wish, a dream, a ring of droplets sparkling in a spider's web after the clouds have passed.

It is rain, running water, the river that floods the valley, urging the lilies to bloom and scouring gold from the beds of gravel and driving the deer to the high mountain meadows where the hunt is made complex by sublimity and spring snow.

The past does not exist.

It is a myth, a dream, a ring of ancient stones on the plain; it is chert, granite, flint; it strikes a spark and the forest burns.

But the trees remember their claim upon the land.

They grow tall and we hew them for timbers to build a home not far from the river, with the mountains in view, planting lilies, sketching clouds, panning for gold, praying for rain, running from fire, fearful of flood, dreaming of deer, wishing on stones.

It is the house of this moment.

We live in it now.

THE PAST

You must surrender your teeth to it,
sign your candied eyes away,
deliver yourself in rings and butterflies
like dough to the baker's oven.

Years of light gone tungsten-silver,
fidelity to a tune no longer heard,
sacks of onions, a toy pony or zebra,
stepping-stones inlaid with marbles,
with blue and yellow tiles in the garden
and the garden whispering,

Come back to the earth, little stones!

And they do. It gives them up.
They are released
from a weakening bond poured ages ago
and shaped in plastic forms.

In the kitchen, and in the shower,
tiles are missing everywhere,
apples taken by October wind.

Red skin, sweet flesh, the nave of the core
like a chalice, like a hidden chapel
and its secret parishioners—the pips, the seeds.

Beneath their mahogany armor, oh
what mischief the seeds have planned.

•

Ritual grew up in sacred play; poetry was born in play and nourished on play; music and dancing were pure play. Wisdom and philosophy found expression in words and forms derived from religious contests. The rules of warfare, the conventions of noble living were built up on play-patterns. We have to conclude, therefore, that civilization is, in its earliest phases, played. It does not come *from* play like a babe detaching itself from the womb: it arises *in* and *as* play, and never leaves it.

—JOHAN HUIZINGA, *Homo Ludens*

•

In Flight, Seattle to Miami

Why pretend that we are blind to history, or it to us?
From 30,000 feet I can feel its metamorphic currents,
cars and trucks inching through workday traffic
along the boulevards and flyovers
of a mid-American city I do not recognize.
The river is green, carving its way among hills.
Low mountains in the distance, color of old grass cuttings.
Farms below with long aluminum-roofed outbuildings—
chicken houses or tobacco sheds—and now
a nest composed of mountains wrinkled as tobacco leaves,
green escarpment ancient and eroded, some Ozark
or Appalachian tier folding into winter-browned farmland,
rifts that read as emergent ribs of a long-buried leviathan
left to rot on the floor of an ancient sea,
wave after wave of ridgeline the roads align with
as the earth's blueprint is accommodated and made real.

From here the continent flows outward in every direction,
a great scarred shield of rock no longer molten
but plastic, elemental, generative, telluric.

A larger river and a plume of steam from a power plant
at the bend below a dam which forms a licorice-black lake
like a jigsaw puzzle among jagged hillsides.

On the in-flight video soldiers are departing for war.

Sailors are tossing small children in the air
while a band plays classic rock aboard the USS *George
Washington*,
a boy is wearing his father's helmet,
a woman in desert camouflage beams at her smiling
infant.

Aggression: from the Latin *aggredi*, "to approach with
hostility."
Ag—"out"—and *gradi*—"to step."
From the Indo-European root: *gredh*, "to walk."

To step out, to arise and go forth, to place one foot
in front of the other,
to walk into the world is to aggress upon it.

•

Civilization has to be defended against the individual, and its regulations, institutions and commands are directed to that task.

—SIGMUND FREUD, *The Future of an Illusion*

•

To say society is to speak of a history that is slow, mute and complicated; a memory that obstinately repeats known solutions, to avoid the difficulty and danger of imagining something else.

—FERNAND BRAUDEL, *Civilization and Capitalism*

•

The life of civilization was for me like a dream from which I tried to wake up in vain. Or—and this is also true—my life was such a dream.

—CZESLAW MILOSZ, *Unattainable Earth*

•

In Flight, Miami to Phoenix

Somewhere over the deep blasted desert.

Snowy mountains far off to the south, must be Mexico,
pinwheels of irrigators in the desolate lands,
a geometry of human desire and earthly intransigence.

Olduvai territory.
An Afghanistan of the soul.

Speaks of origins.

Speaks of deep time, warped striations, chthonic passage.
Speaks of ancient grasslands, the species evolving—
moments when it feels apprehensible.

Speaks of America.
Speaks of horses and thirst.

Speaks as one from whom a testimony
of absolute emptiness has been extracted
by the hoodless torturers of the sun.

PHOENIX

Like toys from a box, shaken out,
bright cars and alphabet blocks
strewn across the floor of the desert.

Like cargo dumped from a plane by accident,
things left out in the sun too long,
grown up planless, and desolate, and ordinary.

Was it the same for the Egyptians,
for the anchorite
crying out in the wilderness,

O Lord, I have passed through the fire
of this life and survived?
Like a blade of grass in your wind, O Lord?

Like a blind man seeking to decipher
with his hands your words
inscribed on tablets of salt amid the downpour.

Amulet of chalk and circuitry,
a city burning
faintly green against the god-bone.

•

Like our bodies and like our desires, the machines we have devised are possessed of a heart which is slowly reduced to embers. From the earliest times, human civilization has been no more than a strange luminescence growing more intense by the hour, of which no one can say when it will begin to wane and when it will fade away. For the time being, our cities shine through the night, and the fires still spread.

—W. G. SEBALD, *The Rings of Saturn*

•

EGYPTOLOGY

Even in that hour the knowledge
that our willful titanism cannot save us,
such prescient constructs no more
than ribbons time itself has braided
in our hair, courses of the river in flood
season after season rewritten
while bedrock glistens unperturbed.

Even chiseled, hawsered, sawn into blocks,
stacked, girdered, engineered, blessed,
it is no more than a division of spoils,
partitions of a hive which may yet
be thrown down from its perch
and burned in coils of scented smoke,
moonfall bitten blue and amoral
across the marmoreal sky
of a descent beyond reckoning,
baubles, buried treasure, canopic jars,
lost process by which we shall know
no home but eternity, no balm
but sweet water in the shade of date palms,
a ringing of earthenware bells,
small foundries forging ingots of tin,
oil lamps along the water where

boys on donkeys proffer cinnamon and figs
beside the granary of the Pharaoh.

Because it lives here, within us, has burned
its fingerprints into the fabric of stars
unspooled from the spinnerets of time
the spider, time the jackal, the ass,
time the healer, the embalmer, the annealer,
the annointer, the vain and destructive,
the intransigent, the incorporeal, the just,
the praiseworthy, the bereaving and bereft—

always the same, witness and vanishing,
ransacked, laid bare, scoured, thirsty,
incorruptible and transformed and always

the same.

We cannot touch it, halt it, name it.

It sails past, wind upon the Nile,
rowed by whom and bound for what shore?

PAPYRUS

NOTEBOOK

Chicago

Lonely daffodils and unbloomed tulips
enduring the frost without complaint.
Bare trees—they seem as if they want to speak
but have, for some reason, stopped themselves,
or been stopped. Muted, silenced, censored.
Or are they speaking to someone else?
Is their message beyond range of my wind-bitten ears,
pitched to the wrong frequency or current,
the wrong chronology or horizon?
Perhaps the trees are talking all the time,
their words evolving over years and decades,
their budding flowers are a message for the bees,
a profuse and ripening script for the clouds,
and leaves are a message, the forest is singing
a collective song that lasts a millennium,
the Earth composes a single sentence
that will unspool until its final hour,
stars, the galaxies, cosmological syntax—.

How can the frost-tinged narcissus not ring
with some echo of what I am feeling?
How can it remain undivided in its loyalty to this world
when the perfect weather of the self beckons,
the isolation of consciousness whirling its own cyclones,
creating its own moon and sun, Ganymede and Io?
Feeling the rock of the planet revolve beneath my feet
I ground myself, I root and identify:
hominid, middle-sized, midcontinent, midlife.
And then the fish of the self swallows the lure
and runs line off the reel like a blood-red balloon
careening its string among these naked elms.
Like reading Rilke as the snow comes down
past the streetlight in the alley, a magical theater,
a dome of sacred inconsequence, the world
moving through its circle of illumination and passing on
as snow, falling. Still falling. Then fallen.

April snow! The boys toss sodden snowballs at trees
and attempt to roll a snowman. Lacking the touch,
they manage only obloid boulders to kick into chunks
and toss into the branches of the crab apple tree.
Beauty of it: shrubs outlined in white, branches given body,
the limbs holding more, each little bud anointed with it.
And then the tall bare maples like fan coral, thickened,
the gradation of branches down to scrimshaw twigs
etching the sepulcher of storm-eyed sky, and then
they lurch into motion, such motions translating
through those final whip-thin attenuations into dance—.
And there's the squirrel, on cue, eating crab apple buds,
spilling snow to the ground with each frolicsome leap.
Birds twittering—they don't seem concerned at all.
There is too much evidence of spring, I suppose,
for this late benediction of winter to worry them.
Snow shovels. Tick-tock. Guys rehabbing the kitchen
two porches over speaking in Polish and Spanish.
Their words bounce off the glinting surfaces and shatter.
Reverb, depth of field. Ideas that burn in the mind!

EXISTENCE

1.

I had forgotten what it was like to exist
this way. I am a different person in Chicago,
a little deeper but sadder, melancholic,
less supple within my own skin.
Strange sense of slippage, returning here,
revisiting former lives and past estates,
as if the film had jumped its sprockets and the gears
of the clattering projector spun to no effect.
Exist in the moment, yes, but the past is inescapable,
the past is oxygen to the blast furnace of being,
uranium to the reactor of consciousness.
Should I say human consciousness?
Is it so different for bees, lemurs, longhorn sheep?
Are consciousness and self precise synonyms?
Can we imagine one without the other?
Can we conceive of consciousness outside of time
or is it a projection of time within us,
consciousness my temporal expression as my body
is my expression in three-dimensional space?

2.

Driving from Miami we stopped to watch the manatees
that shelter all winter in the Homossassa River

and happened upon an island inhabited by monkeys.
There was a sign explaining how they had been pets
of a local eccentric but now lived without interference
on their mangrove-shrouded refuge, kept healthy
by a diet of fresh mangoes and Purina monkey chow.
So the myth of a benevolent, all-providing god.
But what was the monkeys' opinion of their captivity
in the midst of that astonishing, spring-fed river?
Were they aware how much their predicament
resembled our own? Could they feel the current of time
swirling past and around them? Did they even exist?
The sign was hand-lettered, the morning silent,
the story preposterous though hardly impossible.
We saw no monkeys, but what does that prove?

CONSCIOUSNESS

An obsessive compulsion, a ring of keys,
a sequence of numerals to roll the tumblers
and open the golden vault, a web, a blizzard,
a stochastic equation to generate song.
It goes on. There is no satiety mechanism
in the market system, in the agora of thought.
We cannot bloom, cannot flower,
cannot crystallize into coal or diamond
or disassemble ourselves into pure melody.
Alone in the ruined observatory we stand
surrounded by astral bodies, glittering
milk-folds of star creation we stutter to name
but still we cannot burn our fingerprints
into the void. Into. The. Saints of it, myths of it,
cloister, waterwheel, winged lion, myrrh.
Knots of olive wood in a beached rowboat
over which to roast the tiny silver fish
delicious with salt and lemon. Marooned, then,
but well-fed on the substance of this world.
And still forsaken. And still hungry.

RILKE AND GOD

When Rilke talks about God I have no idea
what to say. It's like being buttonholed at a party
by someone who wrongly assumes you share
the urgency of their political convictions,
their devotion to a cause and its glorious leader,
a man of catastrophically dangerous power.
Time to fill your drink, grab some salted almonds.
But then he talks about art in the same voice,
and I come to see that to him they are one
and the same, aspects of an indivisible fire,
facets of a singular jewel, and I can understand
where he is coming from, I have anecdotes
to supply, grievances to air, a savvy joke,
some watercooler wisdom. And so we part
if not as friends, then, contented acquaintances.

3 A.M.

Yes, everything that is truly seen must become a poem.
— RILKE

1.

Worrying the bone of the future into slivers of the past.

Staring out the window at halos of light, the alley trees,
night sounds assembling into tiny monostichic poems,
a hum, knots and blooms, algal minutiae, matchsticks,
    kindling,
ascetic archways rising and falling, telephone lines
that bridge the rainfall to fulfill a promise written in
    filaments.

Zones of thought, mimic-markings, allotments geared to
    suffer,
momentous shapes that seem to belong to another world,
ways of concerning the air like cottonwoods prone to
    flower,
the farthest away waving like a child being kidnapped.

2.

Transparency, and the attrition of falling leaves.
Clemency, and the abstraction of sparrows.
Truancy, and the absolution of stars.

Yellow lilies in a vase on the coffee table—makes me want to find a brush and paint! Haven't felt that impulse in many years. In color-drenched Miami painting seems redundant, like pouring gasoline on a fire. View out the back toward the brick garage, the industrial green alleyway of trash bins, the black tarred roof, gray angles of houses through a screen of bare trees, red brick chimney, a new brass roof coping—that's the whole palette: grays, whites and off-whites, glossy black, matte black, muted brick and muddy ochre, not true red but earthy and organic reds. And there is metal—iron and bright aluminum—and black cables and phone lines, and gray electric cables, and brown utility poles. A grab-bag vernacular of garages, porches, carriage houses, stoops and porticoes. The backs of homes are more revealing than their faces, informal and unscripted, like people on vacation, like reality TV, and the city's alleys compose an urban commons that is actually quite lovely on our block, backyards like a valley between the low cliffs of apartment buildings, the alley a babbling brook upon the valley floor, all the catkins busting out of the bare branches, the forsythia not yet bloomed but already yellow, yellow like a clarion, like an Augustinian text. Color matters in Chicago, every shade and half-tone, silvery gray scale of the rain-wet trees, voluptuous green of tulip shoots, a world of color reassembling, reconfiguring its photons and pix-els. Incipience! Clay at the river's edge as the gods emerge from the water, the winged lion poised above the gates of the city at dawn.

Talking in class about rhetorical posture.
The students, several of whom are extravagantly
gifted, have been so deeply indoctrinated
with the depersonalizing jargon of critical theory
that they can barely accommodate the notion
of authorial agency, let alone the concept of a speaker.
Where is the speaker situated in this poem?
Not the speaker but the voice. Not the voice
but the self. Not the self but the locus of issuance.
How can I convince them that poems if texts
are human texts, that texts if artifacts
are artifacts forged in the furnace
of the heart, the soul, the psyche, however
you imagine or care to name that machine
we hear idling in the engine room at night.
Springlike today, near seventy, sunny and blue.
Budding trees no longer skeletal as logic.
The particular hickory or maple in the alley
whose sheaves of hairline branches engraved
discrete linear designs upon the iridescent sky
has swollen into generality, a fuzzy abstraction.
Another week should see the bloom-out
of purest, whisper-green shoots, darkening
all summer to fall.

If language is a circulatory system of symbols what are
    images but wounds where the blood coagulates as the
    world's infection rushes in?

If consciousness is the subject of the lyric poem, beads of
    a golden abacus calculating a path through time, how
    do you stop the train without derailing it?

If the self is a type of infinite regression are not our
    attempts to escape it, however ingenious, doomed to
    fail?

Why prefer the cloth of chance to the garment of
    identity? Why pay obeisance to the tyranny of the
    random?

To discover suprahuman creativity one need only
    consider a cloud, a flower, the taste of honey, the sound
    of constellations turning.

Nature dwarfs our capacities with contemptuous ease,
    as do the Olympian gods and perhaps the Alpha
    Centaurians gazing down at us with pity and disgust,

but if you were to offer me the fruit of their radiant and
    perfected art I would say, so what?

Of course it is sublime, of course it is ineffable; of course
    they're better than us, bathed as they are in rays of
    harmonic contentment!

Of course we embody oppressive ideologies, of course we
    are flawed—that such confused, furless, greedy,

god-haunted, fear-driven, blood-frenzied animals dare to
    risk the task of creation is itself the justification of the
    act.
Now, what were those dishes Li-Young ordered—chicken
    feet, tripe, whole baby octopus in curry sauce.
    Delicious!
And for dessert, little cubes of gelatin flavored like
    coconut, dry and woody, and like mango, syrupy and
    floral, doused in condensed milk.
We drink five or six pots of tea and hover perhaps two
    feet above the floor watching the voices of the patrons
    floating around us in the form of Chinese ideograms
the way Bugs Bunny sees cartoon birds and musical notes
    when struck on the head with a mallet.

SLEEP

Falling asleep you do not traffic in abstractions:
you fashion images in the mind and count them.
You step back from the brink of thought,
from cognitive manipulation, to pure envisioning.
The sheep jump the wall, the skier parses new trails
on the mountain, swooping between spruce trees.
Elizabeth walks through homes she has known:
an old apartment in Chicago, our beloved hovel
on Jane Street, her childhood house in Baltimore.
What's down this hall, which door is the closet?
Turn on the light, examine the faded wallpaper,
move through the space, feel it, inhabit it.
What's been subtracted is a kind of pictorial syntax,
the filmic and interpretive operations of the mind
driving the images forward. Or, is that wrong?
You must remember to count the leaping sheep,
to engage the algebraic half of the mind,
which is the left or the right? Does it matter?
Two hemispheres, globe and brain,
night and day, the mad serendipity of it all.
What is the evolutionary purpose of sleep?
What is knowledge? Why are we alive?
Where is this world we find ourselves in?
How can we understand it? Who are we?

At the playlot, where we took Sam as an infant to toddle, Jackson says: *It's all about the monkey bars.*

Elizabeth remembers how, long ago, in his ludicrous puffy snowsuit, we had to stuff Sam into the baby swing, like a giant marshmallow.

Sam says: *What's a snowsuit?*

Meanwhile the ivy has come back to life, its brown stitchery against our gray stone walls suddenly flush with velveteen leaves, still unfurling, the color of molten lead, and all the flowering apple and pear trees festooned with petals up and down the block.

INVITATIONS

To rhetoric: quarry me
for the stones of such tombs as may rise
in your honor.

To molecules: let me be carbon.
To the burners of bones: let me be charcoal.

To the drosophila: declaim to me
of finger bananas.

To eyes: that they might look askance
in the darkness and find me.

PAPYRUS

1.

The opposite of sunlight
is not darkness but anti-light,
a mass of ionic occlusion,
seams of which riven
with purple fire illuminate
the parataxis of butterflies
and the dark waters
full of lobsters in migration
like a poetry that moves
from surreal to confessional to
whatever it is it is then.

2.

The code breakers in the end
were revealed to have deciphered
messages that had never been
encrypted. The less said about
that unfortunate situation
the better. $6 + 1 = 9$
is a proposition that refutes
the hierarchical structures
of the old math but not to mean
is a misuse of the medium

and all non-meaning is equally
meaningless. The system,
it turns out, is not substantive
but mediative and translational,
a conjury of rooster bones
and wish fulfillment.

3.

History is continuous
and embraces everything
without exception, wise rule
and waste management,
famine and falling leaves.
We could set out in skiffs
to hunt hippopotami
in the delta marshes
as the Egyptians did
but words do not engage
their meaning. They enable it.
With sharpened sticks
we might yet succeed but
the breeding grounds
are protected by the gods

and that animal is more food
than our village requires.

4.

And then the play is over
and the crew dismantling sets
is drinking too much coffee
and sussing a name for what
is neither hinge nor lever.
Not gloss but habitat.
They live there, like polyps
behind the mirror with
an adhesion defying logic.
Remove the cyclorama
that is language
and you can watch the cogs
and gears revolve
but you must put it back
to describe them.

Again the desire to insert a self between language and the world, between film and screen—bodies garmented in pure light—as though to pry the self loose from consciousness, the observer from the gaze, to pickax a verbal archaeology or remove a cancerous tumor, as the Aztecs knew to wedge the rib cage open and bear forth the beating heart of syntax.

Jacob wrestling the angel
of syntax.

These soldiers died for the honor of syntax.
The stones, the altars, the passage tombs erected in
    homage to syntax.

White tigers in the emporiums of belief,
deep-fried schemata on a bed of field greens.

| bear hunters | cadaver dogs | tulip farmers |
| julep plantations | ionic fields | social orders |

emporia

"they have planted the vitreous floaters in our eyes to monitor our consumption patterns and feed us subliminal advertising for Coke, Budweiser, McDonald's"

Sense of dislocation, relocation, echolocation.

Discovered by bats in the hollow trunk of a sycamore tree. Discovered by cadaver dogs in the stacks at the university.

come climb the library tree with me

Here: the gates of the city.
Here: a new theory of explanation, a new exemplar,
a new contingency,
a new barbarism, bracketed and implicit.
Glyph: rose or lion. Glyph:
the burning bush.
Here: a new form of musical notation,
new grams, new ounces
so we function more efficiently,
a new genealogy, a new modernity.
Glyph: moon and meadow,
wind through the beaded curtain of her hair.
Here: phlox and timothy.
Here: another new contingency, a flower,
a new probity, a new reason.
Glyph: the martyr, the stick figure.
Here: a new uncertainty,
a new littoral,
a community of ruins,
an unreadable nobility, a new dream state.
Here: the unspoken. Here: notes
on the unspoken.
Glyph: fragmentation,
chance and excess,
unsettlement, a gaze, a moderate dependency.

Here: a new usuality, a new haze,
a new phobia, a plea for erasure,
an ethics of stimulus.
Glyph: logos, the hyena, rebirth,
the salvific.
Here: a new catastrophe, a new
poetics of disaster,
a newly authenticated
community of ruins. Glyph: the deaf-mute,
sign and countersign.
Glyph: our
eternal union, emblem
of paradise. Here: nothing.
Here: the gates
of the city.
Glyph: scent of cloves,
something horsed on immortality.
Here: a new triumphalism carved in sandstone,
name of a bird or tree or flower.
Here: name of a bird.
Here: a tree, a flower, a tree.

FORMS OF ATTENTION

Often writing is a kind of listening,
a form of deep attention.
Tuning the stations, fingering the dial.

From whence does that voice arise,
a spring in which foothills?
What will it say next?

The feeling of exhaustion
as one falls back upon the bed,
the sensation of thirst as water passes the lips—

are these forms of attention?
No.
These are harmonies of fulfillment.

What we don't know can't save us,
what we don't dare dream won't.

———

A dream of sour milk, clear and noxious—and the next day I drink the milk and it is sour.

———

Sick for three days, high on cold medicine, full of wild and lucid dreams. Two very strange, language-driven dreams last night. The first concerns "contraction"—that's the key word in the dream, a buzzword repeated by corporate types in a boardroom: inspired by the notion of business mergers, and franchise contraction in baseball, America is forced to "contract" itself into "new cities," for instance Cincinittsburgh.

The second is about evolution, which is revealed by a kind of infomercial narrator to have a "linguistic" basis, as proven by this "scientific equation": *langostino via languor into lemur.*

———

Knowledge like a jewel imperfectly formed
radiates both true and false light.

The ash of language blankets our world.

It is the grit that causes the pearl to form,
the fire that casts the diamond
upward toward the surface of this dream.

———————

Trapped in the body of sleep I remain
a man.
(Ocelot, narwhal, chimp.)

———————

matches in the dark, guttering out

———————

Alone in the Loop all day, ritualized aggression of the marketplace, Chicago River Neptune green—almost summer! Familiar Van Goghs at the Art Institute, Cornell boxes, Hokusai's *Great Wave*. Crocuses, bluebells and snowdrops, daffodils, hyacinth, that knavish dancer. Spring brings spatial resonance to the city, dimensionality, as the branches fill with burrs and leaflets, lambent, spongelike, air becoming aqueous, gelatinous. Not precisely. Oh gee, not feeling well at all. Going to hit the Nyquil again, try to drug myself into restorative slumber.

Long Day's Journey into Nyquil

Jonesing, hep, fixed on diamonds and donuts, the star
vehicle descends. . . .
Hurricane, storm-wheel, the basilisk's eye. . . .
The coriolis effect spinning the Gulf Stream across the
cold Atlantic. . . .
Atlantic, Pacific, the circumpolar Arctic Sea. . . .
Ocean, the ocean, an ocean, some ocean. . . .
Oceanic, just that word, alone on the blank page. . . .
Oceanic, just like that. . . .

oceanic

Early birds are chirping away—it's three, no it's past four
in the morning! Moving quietly around the apartment,
staring out the windows—the cool spring has kept the
flowers on the trees. Pleasure of deciduous trees! Their
voluminousness. Is that a word? Their volume, compared
to palms. Palm trees are more nearly related to modern
grasses than to deciduous trees, they are giant atavisms,
dinosaurian leaves of grass. Which suggests Walt Whit-
man roaming the South Shore of Long Island as a boy,
learning to name the reeds and rushes. If I have learned
one thing about art it is this: do not question the muse.
Take what is offered. Of grapes, make wine; of blueber-
ries, pie. Dawn purpling the sky, clouds like oak beams.
Civilization as a kind of Einsteinian dream state, every-
thing is one fabric, all of it, this stuff, all the actors and
agents, the void, time and space, wind, rain, body parts
and their greaved desire for union, mortar and pestle,
fields of wheat or rice, tribal gods, religious rituals, echoes
of chaos given form, a random cascading being-in-time, or
time-having-been-lived-through, that arrow, that fecund
imagination, that universal city. This is this and this is
also this. Or that. Or both. It happens. It happens and it is
the having-happenedness of it that matters, past and fu-
ture, time like a process, an engine, a seed. Which sug-

gests Po Chü-i, in his southern exile, passing his days drinking wine and writing poems, planting lilies on the western face of the mountain. It is a garden, an inception. We can start with that.

LATE SPRING

The kingdom of perception is pure emptiness.
—PO CHÜ-I

1.

I have faltered in my given duty.
It is a small sacrilege, a minor heresy.

The nature of the duty is close attention
to the ivy and its tracery on riled brick,

the buckled sidewalk, the optimistic fern,
downed lilacs brown as coffee grounds,

little twirled seedwings falling by the thousands
from the maples in May wind,

and the leaves themselves
daily greener in ripening sunlight.

To whom is their offering rendered,
and from whom derived,

these fallen things
urging their bodies upon the pavement?

There is a true name for them,
a proper term, but what is it?

2.

Casting about, lachrymose, the branches
of the trees at 4 a.m.

flush with upthrust flowers,
like white candles in blackened sconces.

All day I was admonished
to admire the beauty of this single peony

but only now, in late starlight,
do I crush its petals to my face.

Elemental silk dimmed to ash,
reddening already to the brushstroke of dawn,

its fragrance is a tendril
connecting my mind to the rain,

a root, a tap, a tether.
Such is the form of the duty,

but which is its officer,
the world or the senses?

The many languages of birds now,
refusing to reconcile,

and clouds streaming out of the darkness
like ants to the day's bound blossom.

DAWN

NOTEBOOK

Barnegat Light, New Jersey

I have itemized the starry night, dare I
attempt the cloudless dawn?
— WALT WHITMAN, *Specimen Days*

DAWN

5 a.m.: the frogs
ask what is it, what is it?
It is what it is.

Dawn. Across the inlet at the state park the mobile homes are silhouetted with eerie clarity against a low horizon of volcanic red shading to rose then a pencil mustache of backlit clouds, bark gray, then peach-flesh whitening through lemon candy to the now blue dome—barest, night-heaviest blue, weighty and necessary, like a cardiac surgeon donning a robe as she enters the operating theater. Boats are going out—not the scallop boats, not the commercial fleet already at sea in pursuit of tuna or fluke or whichever silvery indeterminate fish, but the loud-revved joyboats of the Jerseyites. Must be Saturday. Lost track of the days already. On this side of the water all is calm. In the shadow of the lighthouse only the breakfast places will be humming at this hour—Andy's, Kelly's, Mustache Bill's, the Coffee Shack. They could be Whitman's, all these tall grasses and reeds—they are his, I suppose, this must resemble his Paumanok a hundred and fifty years ago. Sea oats, cattails, calamus—maybe Jackson will learn to distinguish them at marine biology camp and teach me. Songs and hosannas rising from the bushes, invisible, to greet the sun. Too many birds: tern, gull, sparrow, I know the commonplace but not the exotics. Why am I awake? Green beacon on the jetty, pulsing. Clouds now aflame, revealing their depth—back to the horizon they run, gaining a third dimension, riffled and corrugated in steely gray and hot pink. A big two-masted schooner under sail far out on the horizon—now inching directly behind the tiny mobile homes so that the tips of its tall sails sit atop them like spectators at a stock car race or coronation or the burning of an unlucky heretic. Auto-da-fé. The sun. It's coming. Now the overarching clouds are full with it, replete, grave, rain-heavy with its radiance. Bright lucent orange, narrowly contained, embryonic—even someone with no knowledge of this world, or planets, or orbits, or dawn, even a flatworm would know that something amazing was happening, that a great power is lurking, impending, that it will rise, rises, is rising—as they always knew, the cairn-builders, scriveners in paint and animal hide—a gull chuckles, where is he?—I turn back to its emergence, now rapidly it comes, half a circle, more—the sweet cool pearly light of my reeds will be lost! The crickets are dropping off, the frogs, a brave few keep up the racket. The low trills and calls of birds, cheeps, cackles, whoop-o-wheeps—could that be a whippoorwill, do we have those in New Jersey?—and the steady note of the foghorn, though it is clear.

•

You must not know too much, or be too precise or scientific about birds and trees and flowers and watercraft; a certain free margin, and even vagueness—perhaps ignorance, credulity—helps your enjoyment of these things, and of the sentiment of feather'd, wooded, river or marine Nature generally. I repeat it—don't want to know too exactly, or the reasons why. My own notes have been written off-hand in the latitude of middle New Jersey. Though they describe what I saw—what appear'd to me—I dare say the expert ornithologist, botanist or entomologist will detect more than one slip in them.

—WALT WHITMAN, *Specimen Days*

•

EARLY JULY

Showering outside
by candle glow: too lazy
to change the lightbulb.

Jellyfish season—
climbing back into this world
alive and tingling.

Alone on the beach,
one kite and me, drinking beer.
Sunset, July 1st.

THE BEACH

Beach chairs in the surf
so the moms don't have to move—
long day at the beach.

Jackson says it's like
a mad symphony today,
the sound of the waves.

Beach chairs rotating
around shade umbrellas like
sundial shadows.

Warm water—the smell
of Florida! The Gulf Stream,
blown west, waves hello.

Seaweed: someone says
it's like swimming in salad—
long day at the beach.

A crab bit my foot yesterday, a blue claw, in the late afternoon surf, as I waited for waves on the sandbar. The cut is red-lipped and painful, even after hours soaking in the sea. Same green, glass-flat ocean today, water clear and clean—vast numbers of coquinas at low tide—waves not as big but curling perfectly at the bar, more of a shelf, a flat plateau of sand, some sea lettuce floating around, but not the vast sheaves of eelgrass. And there were rays in the surf, their white underbellies in the curling wave, wingtips breaking the surface, a whole bunch of them (flock, herd, school, flotilla), several dozen, swimming with us, unafraid. They must have been feeding on the smorgasbord of that sandy table—everywhere underfoot countless mussels, pebble-sized coquinas, clams, a few scallops, moon snails—the boys identify their orange, glassy "doors," which should better be called shoes, as they cover their feet—and a zillion mangled crab parts, claws, legs, guts and shreds from blue and green and calico crabs, Japanese crabs, spider crabs, horseshoe crabs, churned and broken bodies of crabs, and little schools of killifish and silversides, and the rays, feeding.

JULY 9

5 a.m.

Dark. Dark, but alive. Energized, expectant. Turbo-charged darkness. When does the first note of precolor appear? Impossible to delineate. There it is. Tear in the fabric, suture in gauze. Long minutes of paling, lightening—bruised, coal-infused, color-free. Then the Flemish grays and now, almost, a blue, where two fat stars hang in the east—companions at the slow birth of day, midwives—I should know their names.

A painter revealing the canvas—
ah, charcoal clouds in thumb-smudged impasto.
White sand picks up the first note of light, heather balds
    and dune slopes.

What is the name of the morning star?

Fishing boats heading out the inlet
with the lighthouse and Venus standing watch.

    The paling of night
    becomes dawn; Venus withdraws
    behind her curtain.

5:15

Two processes: dawn, then sunrise. Dawn emerges from night through semidark grayscale to a palette of neonatal pinks, violets and oranges, with umber clouds. Sunrise is a forge, a steelworks. Violent silvers, reds, and the big star of the show, Sol, on fire, radiant and prolific.

> Ah, here comes the star
> of our show now, our one and
> only star—the sun.

5:20

A kind of hushed dawn today. No wind. Single fishing boat coming in with red running lights still on. Fog-horn sounding. Crickets. Subdued bird twitter—not yet airborne. Counting syllables, dollars, observations this morning. Diurnal calculations. The porch is nineteen boards across. Yellow rubber cutout starfish, water-sod-den. Sun-faded baby pool half full of rainwater. Over-turned child's chair. Brown Astroturf-type floor mat. Blue baby swing suspended on yellow ropes from eyehooks in the crossbeam—I screwed them in, crooked, for Sam, how many years ago? Plastic bass fishing "casting practice" target. Multicolored hammock from Honduras. Boogie boards, skim boards. Standard-issue white plastic outdoor chairs from Wal-Mart. Burned matches. Cigarette butts. Diet Coke can. Rubber band. Ant. Leaf in spiderweb. Sand, pebbles. Assorted clothes hung over railing, salt-stiffened T-shirts, bathing suits turned inside out. Green garden hose looped over railing.

5:30

The birds come in now, as dawn really gets established. Chromatic red, cherry-Slurpee red. Horizon half screened by purple clouds; whole thing filtered—the light would otherwise be yellow and full by now.

Watched over by friends,
Venus and the old lighthouse,
fishing boats at dawn.

5:40

Show in full swing. More fishing boats.
Turn off the reading lamp—surrender to sunlight.
Bleaching now. Sense of loss.
Why am I awake?

Still time to jump back in bed before the kids wake up.
A little green bug on the carpet—where is it headed, at
    this hour,
off to work, or home to the family?
Still time—.

5:45

Go.

READING WALT WHITMAN AT DAWN

Wakened by the sound
of feet on the porch I find
two sparrows, hopping!

What is the dune grass
trying to do—praise the sun
or go back to sleep?

Friendly grasshopper,
tell me the name of that bird
and I'll sing with you.

BEAUTY

Beauty of this world—
walked six miles along the beach,
counting syllables

Beauty of this world,
starlight on the salt meadow—
ah, the moon is full!

Beauty of this world
and the foghorn bemoaning
its mortality.

Cool and foggy. Weeks are zooming past—not even keeping track of things, nothing but haiku. Where did our beautiful summer go? The steady winds move the warm surface water offshore and as the deep waters of the North Atlantic rise up the surf temperature drops nearly twenty degrees in two days. Deep abyssal cycle of Arctic waters, the buried canyons, the lost world of the ocean floor. Sam studied this in science last year—I remember quizzing him before the test. On the empty beach Elizabeth and I hunch into our sweatshirts and windbreakers to watch the boys' surfing lessons. Can't believe Jackson can endure the freezing water—59 degrees today! I try to swim but can hardly stand it; my face burns; Miami has ruined me. Jackson is so small and agile he can basically run up and down the big blue longboard Paul is teaching them on—I am tempted to describe him as capering like a wild monkey as he rides the afterwash in to shore. Sam is catching real waves, learning to gauge the break, turn and paddle and rise. All the time Paul stands chest deep in the cold: burly, Australian, a former lifeguard, his movie star good looks a fringe benefit Elizabeth enjoys—he married a local girl and now gives surfing lessons in summer and works as a commercial fisherman all winter, hauling fluke on his brother-in-law's boat. A thoughtful, steady teacher, though only winter storms bring waves big enough to interest him; his wife displays the photo of a tiny figure surfing an enormous wave—Paul in his Arctic wetsuit, with hood and gloves and booties, the beach covered in snow.

QUESTIONS

Middle of July—
what better for breakfast now
than blueberry pie?

Visitors tonight—
who will bike to the market
for swordfish and corn?

Elizabeth asks,
what's up with this haiku thing?
Pinecones in the sand.

•

One bright December mid-day lately I spent down on the New Jersey sea-shore, reaching it by a little more than an hour's railroad trip over the old Camden and Atlantic. I had started betimes, fortified by nice strong coffee and a good breakfast (cook'd by the hands I love, my dear sister Lou's—how much better it makes the victuals taste, and then assimilate, strengthen you, perhaps make the whole day comfortable afterwards). Five or six miles at the last, our track enter'd a broad region of salt grass meadows, intersected by lagoons, and cut up everywhere by watery runs. The sedgy perfume, delightful to my nostrils, reminded me of the "mash" and south bay of my native island. I could have journey'd contentedly till night through these flat and odorous sea-prairies. From half-past 11 till 2 I was nearly all the time along the beach, or in sight of the ocean, listening to its hoarse murmur, and inhaling the bracing and welcome breezes. First, a rapid five-mile drive over the hard sand—our carriage wheels hardly made dents in it. Then after dinner (as there were nearly two hours to spare) I walk'd off in another direction (hardly met or saw a person), and taking possession of what appear'd to have been the reception-room of an old bathhouse range, had a broad expanse of view all to

115

myself—quaint, refreshing, unimpeded—a dry area of sedge and Indian grass immediately before and around me—space, simple unornamented space. Distant vessels, and the far-off, just visible trailing smoke of an inward bound steamer; more plainly, ships, brigs, schooners, in sight, most of them with every sail set to the firm and steady wind.

—WALT WHITMAN, *Specimen Days*

•

THE BEACH

Skimboarding, I fall—
yo, bring back the board, numbnut.
I'm too old for this.

Bodysurfing—now
that the waves and we are spent
I need a beer. Two.

Sand castles, low tide—
the clams give their shells to dig
a future Venice.

Sand castles, low tide,
throwing footballs in the waves—
need another line.

Very hot, hazy,
big crowds at the beach all day.
Not much to report.

ZODIAC NARRATIVE

Crossing low water
the Zodiac runs aground—
sorry, razor clams.

Crossing low water
the boys carry driftwood swords
to slay their uncle.

Crossing low water
to sandbars, mid-bay, alone
with terns and willets.

Crossing low water
Sam falls overboard and laughs
at himself all day.

DAYS OF LATE JULY

Silver maples flash
their underbellies in wind—
days of late July.

Shells full of spare change
on the dresser—the silver
days of late July.

LATE JULY, AFTER THREE DAYS OF RAIN

Three-day storm—something
for the housebound chickadees
to gossip about.

Three days of weather,
baby pool full of raindrops,
three days of cartoons.

Even gulls disdain
these pretzel goldfish floating
in the baby pool.

Just turning 5 a.m. Hard to see anything—the sky a pale melon swath, cantaloupe over blue smoke. Scattered clouds above, almost an olive drab, and ash, in a bleaching, bluing, broken-boned sky. Engine noise from the inlet—boat going out. Mad cheeping of birds from the meadow and wetlands. White light of the jetty beacon, vivid green light of the shoal beacon, blinking. Peaceful and still after drenching rain and winds all yesterday.

Fell asleep making haiku—but what were they?

> The redwing blackbird
> makes little headway against
> a northeast wind.

Short one syllable.

All the yuccas on the berm flowering this year—because of the unnaturally wet June? Their tall spikes are lonely verticals in a horizontal landscape. And the rambling roses climbing the pine trees, in blossom all July. Should be a poem in those. Only one fishing boat so far. Flutter of wings near at hand—bird on the porch upstairs, gull or blue jay? Going in to Philadelphia next week, just Elizabeth and I, a night away from the family—like a human lifetime. Clouds hard against the horizon line, and a drawn-out lightening process, a flensing, stripping the flesh from the sky's soft bones. Almost-cantaloupe has broadened and dulled into a wan, sickly color, fingers stained with nicotine, yellowed teeth aspiring to aged ivory. Sound of a car on the road. Is that yesterday's storm out there over the ocean? Kind of a stale ice-cream color now, French vanilla partially thawed then refrozen, and battleship gray below that, and above the widening sky-cathedral, growing volumetrically in sea grays, barely blue at all, but spatial now, differentiated. Where are all the reds, oranges and purples today?

Screen door left open—
killing mosquitoes. Issa
would not approve!

Looks like the world is being assembled out of primary elements—metal, clay, water. Ice. Ash. Coal. Sound of a military jet headed for the base in the pine barrens. A little yellower now, like wax beans or lemon-flavored Italian ice. Dawn. The birds, grasses. Sound of the ocean carried on the wind across the dunes. Sky the color of raw titanium.

This is better:

Screen door ajar, so
now I'm killing mosquitoes.
Forgive me, Issa!

Heavy odor of water—dark wet ground, wet sand, wet wood
of the porch, odor of the plants and grasses. No trouble
writing by natural light now, sunlight seeping around the
cusp, like rose petals strewn before the Sultan. Only 5:25!
I would have sworn much longer had passed. Porch still
junked up with flip-flops, squirt guns, a sodden cardboard
box, the baby swing tangled around a beam—always a new
baby in the family, little nephews and the occasional niece,
another cousin on the conveyor belt. Someone is learning
to crawl, someone is learning to read, someone is learning
to surf. Everyone older, but the curve favors those at the bot-
tom over those at the top, and we are stuck in the middle. I
would call it daylight now. 5:31 and the clouds have caught
the angled sunlight and their rippled undersides are bright,
electric pink, o ho! What were faint stains on the night's
fabric have grown into cavernous vaults, curve of the earth
projected in strung-out cirrostratus, proof of planetary ge-
ometry. The spectrum is rounding out, liquid rose losing its
edge to halogen-colored daylight. Show's over. Miraculous
world created anew, as by hand of a master jeweler, like a
seahorse fashioned from flame, gold leaf, salt, and jonquils.

•

There is a dream, a picture, that for years at intervals (sometimes quite long ones, but surely again, in time) has come noiselessly up before me, and I really believe, fiction as it is, has enter'd largely into my practical life—certainly into my writings, and shaped and color'd them. It is nothing more or less than a stretch of interminable white-brown sand, hard and smooth and broad, with the ocean perpetually, grandly, rolling in upon it, with slow-measured sweep, with rustle and hiss and foam, and many a thump as of low bass drums. This scene, this picture, I say, has risen before me at times for years. Sometimes I wake at night and can hear and see it plainly.

—WALT WHITMAN, *Specimen Days*

•

NIGHT THOUGHTS

3 a.m: cheep, cheep.
I, too, sing of happiness—
but I still can't sleep.

Why say happiness?
Ghost clouds sailing past the moon,
sad and immortal.

Whisper of ground mist.
Find contentment where you can.
Whisper of ground mist.

AUGUST

August. Golden haze.
Nights the flesh reawakens
to its selfish dream.

August. Pewter fog
as the storm cell hits: hailstones
hiss in boiling surf.

August. Black scallops
and clamshells in a red pail:
gathered, forgotten.

Cloudy, the foghorn, clacking buoys in the mist. People are
    napping, music is playing dimly through headphones
unattended on the desk while birds risk short cursive
    flights up from the safety of the beach plum thicket.
Six inches of tannic water in the deep-grooved tractor
    marks, rutted paths across sand dunes clothed in
    morning glory,
grass and rushes the color of tarnished brass, like a
    melancholy Van Gogh, the late northern paintings of
    wheat fields.
La tristesse durera toujours, he is reported to have said on his
    deathbed. Undoubtedly true. But happiness may also
    last.
Turn over the rocks, seek it, moment to moment, day to
    cloudiest day, a ring of tombstones, flagpoles in the
    snow—.
Is it worth it? Does the possible joy outweigh the
    inevitable sorrow? What is the point of the question?
Learning to recognize patterns: wakefulness, the
    foghorn, a book of Van Gogh sketches in shroud-light.
The half-repainted refrigerator stands in the middle of the
    floor on newspapers, toll of solitary bells in the mist,
green and red lights of the channel markers, incoming
    fishing boats, dragonflies above the salt marsh,
    shimmering.

Late dinner at a dark café blocks from Rittenhouse Square, iron pots of mussels and Belgian beer and a waiter eager to snag the check and clock out. Such are the summer pleasures of his work—winding down to a glass of red wine, catching the windowed reflection of a girl as she passes, counting the take upon the bar, thick roll of ones and fives, palming the odd ten smooth against zinc and polished walnut, the comforting dinginess of American money, color of August weeds in a yard of rusting appliances, hard cash, its halo of authority, the hands' delight in its fricatives and gutturals, its growl, its purr, gruff demotic against the jargon of paychecks on automatic deposit with Social Security deductions and prepaid dental, realism vs. abstraction, a gallery of modest canvases, more landscapes than still lifes, steeples of the old city with masts and spars, a vista of water meadows with fishermen hauling nets in the distance, women collecting shellfish in wicker panniers. It yields enough to sustain us, after all, the ocean of the past. We've paid. The waiter pockets his final tip and throws down his apron and walks out into the warm night of dogs splashing in public fountains and couples on benches beneath blossoming trees and soon enough we follow, arm in arm across the cobblestones, looking for a yellow cab to carry us into the future.

Someone is making a shopping list at the counter by the window.

Someone is peeling cucumbers, drinking a blue margarita.

Someone rubs a thumb across the tip of a new tooth.

Someone is skidding their bike in the stones at the harbor beneath the signs for the party fishing boats: ALL-DAY FLUKE, HALF-DAY BLUES.

Someone throws a pencil down angrily, someone is eating potato chips from the bag, someone is not eating their Cocoa Krispies.

Someone is picking broken crayons from the washing machine, someone is clicking bottle caps in a palm.

Someone checks her e-mail.

Someone cries.

Someone dives into a huge green wave.

Someone is licking dry salt from a shoulder, shuddering.

Someone feels very alone, and scared.

Someone is expecting FedEx to deliver a new contract, keep your eye open.

Someone is too small to ride the roller coaster, maybe next year.

Someone is throwing pinecones at toy soldiers, someone goes crabbing and catches nothing but eelgrass.

Someone is lying in the hammock, reading a wonderful book.

Someone's hand shadows an egret, lifting olives from
   a porcelain plate, believing the evening swifts are
   whistling just for him.
Someone detects the flavor of flint in the sauvignon
   blanc, flavor of mint, lemon, Irish river gravel.
Someone is studying the *Audubon Field Guide*, someone is
   missing the jingle of absent keys.
Someone is choosing the blueberry over the strawberry-
   rhubarb pie.
Someone deadheads the begonias, someone waters the
   new pink hydrangea, someone's back aches from
   planting.
Someone ordered from the wrong pizza place again!
Someone stacks and unstacks clamshells in the darkness.
Someone wants to hear another story.
Someone pushes the baby stroller down to the inlet,
   buys a coffee at Andy's, watches the boats sail into the
   distance.
Someone wakes in a sweat—it was only a dream!
Someone is in the shower, shouting—*can you bring me a
   towel?*
Someone waits for the beach tractor, kicking at sand,
   bored and happy at the same time.
Someone has had the best year of his life, someone is
   wrestling tempestuous angels.

Someone wraps a smooth rock in seaweed and imagines it
is a dragon egg.
Someone is listening to thunder resound off the ocean
after midnight.
Someone watches her mother's brow, creased with the
labor of memory: was there a shopping list, what was
on the list, where is the list now?

CONSOLATION

Sadness, not sorrow—
like the blue beneath the black
of the mussel shell.

MID-AUGUST

An ant to the stars
or stars to the ant—which is
more irrelevant?

Ninety-six—too hot
to run the grill at Cheryl's,
no cheese steaks today!

Weekend Jet Skiers—
rude to call them idiots,
yes, but facts are facts.

What happy accident has brought this dawn notebook into the world? Why have these haiku chosen me as their instrument? Why am I awake again? Sunlight, circadian rhythms, the sound of the ocean. Summer. Time away from the world and its attachments. Surrounded by family. The beach, the waves. Books. The palette of this coast. A cooler cast of light. Sitting at my desk all morning, Sam at junior lifeguard training, Jackson netting seahorses at marine biology camp, cousins playing in the sand, the house cycling through its routine, listening for the twins to wake from their nap, sorting through thoughts and images, prospecting, turning over rocks to look for poems. Later, walking out along the jetty with the boys, picking through the tide pools, searching for baby crabs. What are the fishermen catching today? Air and seaweed. Someone pulls up a nice flounder but, taking it off the hook, drops it between the giant boulders of the jetty, out of reach. Catch and release. Freed, but not saved. Last night, watching its claws scrabble in the paper bag, Isaac wanted to keep one of the lobsters as a pet—but we ate him, slathered in butter, with fresh corn and sliced tomatoes. The lobster, not cousin Isaac. At the end of the jetty the air is rank and salty and the beach is full of jellyfish, huge quahog shells, mangled horseshoe crabs the seagulls fight over. Driftwood. Not much trash. The dunes are fenced off to protect the nesting grounds of the terns and skimmers, the piping plover. If you walk to the wire they rise up and make a terrible racket. Once, twenty years ago, jogging on the beach—it must have been winter and Elizabeth and I were down from Manhattan for the weekend—I came around a bend and a flock of gulls, the huge ones, great black gulls, caught by surprise, struggled to take flight, rising into a heavy headwind which held them in place all around me as I ran, silently, ears full of music, through and among them, like a galaxy unfurling. All this was underwater then. And my feet did not hurt. Twenty years ago the Army Corps of Engineers constructed the jetty to protect the inlet, and sand accumulated year by year in its lee, and dune grass took root, weeds, creepers, followed by reeds and cattails, bayberry, beach plum, and now cedar and silver maple, the dunes growing larger each year, more birds nesting, even pelicans and ospreys. What was ocean floor is beach and salt marsh. Could the old Maritime Forest return to recolonize it all, could it reemerge from its last, secret groves in the dune hollows behind the lighthouse, deep in stillness, silent, atavistic, enduring? Which is the more unlikely journey, from ocean floor to where we are now, or from here to that forest of ancient holly trees, live oak, black cherry, sassafras?

•

The attractions, fascinations there are in sea and shore! How one dwells on their simplicity, even vacuity! What is it in us, arous'd by those indirections and directions? That spread of waves and gray-white beach, salt, monotonous, senseless—such an entire absence of art, books, talk, elegance—so indescribably comforting, even this winter day—grim, yet so delicate-looking, so spiritual—striking emotional, impalpable depths, subtler than all the poems, painting, music I have ever read, seen, heard. (Yet let me be fair, perhaps it is because I have read those poems and heard that music.)

—WALT WHITMAN, *Specimen Days*

•

Low tide, coquinas
awash in every footprint—
this beach is alive!

Low tide, coquinas
feeding in every footprint—
can't eat my toes, though.

Color is the key to the coquina's inordinate beauty, a variegated palette which leans toward taupe, ivory, cinnamon and a host of washed-out purples ranging from contusion to blueberry via nettle, clover flower, torn jeans and blue slate, but also includes butternut and lemon meringue, underwater brown, raw ochre, p-p-pink! savage tan and old bone, stale coconut and Swiss cheese, watery limeade and bolt-from-the-blue azure, color of sea glass from an old 7UP bottle, color of tangerine peel left five days in the sun, color of anodized aluminum in a thunderstorm, and countless mineral shades—flint, riverstone, chert, granite—and the many compounds and composite variations thereof, tourmaline plus tiger-stripe and unpolished opal, striated chickpea and rusted metal pipe, rainbow mercurochrome and melted Creamsicle. I believe the coquina is my favorite creature, elemental and complex, radiant and benign, filtering invisible nutrients from the

water in its peaceful, heterogenous cities at the tide line—
like a dreamy, subversive, utopian Florida. Jackson and
Ben and Isaac and Cheo collect them in watery holding
pens, amassing huge quantities, which they want to take
home to play with, and when I say no they say not to play
with but "to study." I finally agree to take home a few, in a
bucket of sand and water, and on the way home the boys
ask them questions—"Ever ride in a car before, coquina?
Ever see a tree before?"

Low tide, summer dusk,
footprints of coquinas faint
as constellations.

Dawn, tide rolling huge breakers down the inlet while,
    somewhere, surfers are up already, reading the ocean's
    text.

Why does that feel important, worth protecting, that
    convivial freedom, that tranquillity, that otter-fluid
    grace?

How many times have Elizabeth and I watched late-night
    surfing shows and slept, in the afterglow, like ocean-
    rocked babies?

Hawaii or Australia, a paradisal beach in Fiji or Malaysia—
    Neruda in Rangoon, temple bells and doves!—

exoticism, yes, but I can feel its rhythm on the sandbar,
    whether we bodysurf for hours or idly inhabit the
    space,

floating, talking, buoyed and engrossed. It is about otters,
    the instinct to play, to invent new games—*homo ludens*—

to throw dice against solitude and despair—ha, we shall
    have a brotherhood despite you, o death!—

a type of transcendence I am eager to believe in, a myth I
    hunger to enshrine, like the myth of California,

though this is New Jersey, hazy sun barely risen above
    sandy flats of bayberry and waving reeds.

Somewhere, surfers are up already, driving the coast,
    tramping the dunes in dawn light, looking for waves.

LATE AUGUST

Nephews, cousins, sons—
carrying sleeping children
room to moonlit room.

For this next image
I'd like to thank Robert Hass:
beach towels in moonlight.

Rain at 3 a.m.,
running to close the windows—
no haiku in it.

·

Aug. 22, 1876. . . . Let me say more about the song of the locust, even to repetition: a long, chromatic, tremulous crescendo, like a brass disk whirling round and round, emitting wave after wave of notes, beginning with a certain moderate beat or measure, rapidly increasing in speed and emphasis, reaching a point of great energy and significance, and then quickly and gracefully dropping down and out. Not the melody of the singing-bird—far from it; the common musician might think without melody, but surely having to the finer ear a harmony of its own: monotonous—but what a swing there is in that brassy drone, round and round, cymballine—or like the whirling of brass quoits.

—WALT WHITMAN, *Specimen Days*

·

THE PAST

All day in the waves,
the boys tireless as seals—
mirror of my youth.

Forty: not too old
to eye the Jersey girls but
too old to get caught!

Body of a moth
dismantled by ants—gray skies,
rain all afternoon.

The long rusty dredge boat plying the inlet back and forth all day. Not sure when it arrived, ghostlike, sometime between dawn and breakfast, to clear the channel until dusk. Getting near the end of the season—the deli stops restocking its shelves, White's grocery closes in a week, not much left but potato chips, laundry detergent, unwanted tomatoes in a cardboard box. Flannel shirts appear in the Surf City Five & Dime, the flip-flops are tossed in cartons, headed for the stockroom. The tractor that trundles across the dunes to the beach laden with swimmers has stopped—we'll miss its services—no, here comes the tractor, getting a late start. It must run through Labor Day, as is sensible. About 2 p.m. a huge cloud of starlings rises up from the dunes, the sedge, chittering and twirling in a helical funnel cloud, a vortex, as if scared up by something, or just, what, chasing dragonflies, frolicking? The waves today, stirred up by a hurricane a thousand miles south, are gargantuan—nine, ten feet, rising up and pitching over suddenly at the bar, twenty yards from shore. The afterwash charges up the beach and over the rim, pushing the high tide line back, soaking the towels of unwary families. No, I will not allow Sam to surf—even the sunbleached lifeguard, Bill, after catching a single wave, and being crushed by the next, gives in to the storm surge. We let the undertow drag us out into the foaming swash, then pummel us back up the incline. Jackson builds a sand castle with his cousins. The twins jump around, topple over in the waves, scream, wait to get bigger. Moon jellyfish: like thick transparent saucers of gelatin. Like a sea of silicone breast implants. The force of the waves has pulverized most of them into globules so that, swimming a few strokes, you hit a patch where the water resembles tapioca pudding, grimace, and call it a day.

END OF AUGUST, DAWN

Still don't know their names,
these two stars watching dawn with
such ambivalence.

A dream for winter—
taste of pan-fried soft-shell crabs
and blueberry pie!

What else can I say?
Even the clouds know me now,
risen and burning.

·

It will illustrate one phase of humanity anyhow; how few of life's days and hours (and they not by relative value or proportion, but by chance) are ever noted. Probably another point too, how we give long preparations for some object, planning and delving and fashioning, and then, when the actual hour for doing arrives, find ourselves still quite unprepared, and tumble the thing together, letting hurry and crudeness tell the story better than fine work.

—WALT WHITMAN, *Specimen Days*

·

SUNSET

Clamor of seabirds
as the sun falls—I look up
and ten years have passed.

HURRICANE

NOTEBOOK

Record season of hurricane misery and we are home to endure it. Boarding up, moving the patio chairs into the garage, stacking the potted plants in corners, orchid baskets plucked from the branches. Even as the storm approaches the laundry must get done! And then it has passed, tail end of the serpent sidewinding up the coast,

and already another named system is battering Jamaica,

and we reside within the cone of its probable destiny, and the storm shutters stay up,

and we remain in dusk-light, awaiting landfall.

Checking the house for damage, palm fronds, pinecones, twigs and branches, nothing serious. No mosquitoes! Not one. The wind has literally blown them away, though I can see their larvae wriggling toward the surface of the pools in the hearts of the bromeliads, small wells of tropical misfortune. The fountain in the courtyard is gunked with fallen blossoms, the street is littered with coconuts and mud.

Today the homeless cats in the yard resemble more than ever

the small lions they are.

JACKS

Steady wind from the east, foretelling,
believe it or not, another hurricane,
one of those that circle aimlessly,
appears headed harmlessly out to sea,
then curlicues like a pig's tail before
beelining for lovely Florida. Who is it
now—Gina, Leonardo, Peggy Sue?
Water choppy, strong current ripping
south along the beach. After a while
we see, approaching from the north,
dark patches in the swells, like cloud
shadows or seaweed but it is fish,
clumps and schools and swarms of them,
here come six at a time, then a dozen,
a hundred, a thousand thrashing
the surface as they approach,
surging and swirling around us—
ow!—Elizabeth jumps on my back
as a fish tickles her foot. What kind
of fish are these? Silver with a tail
broadly forked and trimmed in black,
five inches long. A type of jack?
I will look it up at home. Now I am
home. I look it up. They are jacks.

HUMILITY

Sweeping the mud from the courtyard,
mopping the water that's flooded the garage.
A mess, though it might have been far worse.
Upstate two million are without electricity
and suddenly the historical emptiness
of this place comes clear—turn off the juice,
unplug the A/C, and it would revert
in weeks to low-slung jungle. The jungle knows
its place because whatever grows tall
gets knocked down by the wind.
No palm trees here like the slender beanstalk
giants towering over Los Angeles.
Hurricanes teach you to keep your head low.
They teach humility.

Hurricane! Last two days preparing for the worst, battening and re-battening, and then the symbolic eyewall takes a merciful jog on the weather map, forging its way ashore one county to the north. Still we are pummeled, electricity gone, and then, midstorm, a phone call from Elizabeth's parents' condominium building—their windows have blown open, could we please come up and do something about it? So we drive up Collins Avenue in a fury of lashing rain and dangling phone lines, lawn chairs tossed from high-rise balconies into the street, and close their windows, and mop out bucket after bucket of rain. At least we have power up here, to follow the storm on the Weather Channel, and watch *SpongeBob*, and look out from fifteen stories across the eerie, gorgeous, wind-racked ocean, magnesium-blue breaking to sand-scoured alabaster, clouds yawing past and racing out to sea, their gusts knocking the tops from the incoming swells and sending counterwaves pulsing and undulating back across the surface, so the beach is not even eroding too badly, and the coconut palms lay their fronds toward the water like women bending at the waist to wash their hair. Around 7 p.m. we're watching a DVD—*Hellboy*—when three surfers show up; they've dodged police to risk the big storm only to find a flat and unsurfable sea. The clouds are so low overhead, streaming in banner-thin regiments from the northwest to the southeast. Howl of the windows rattling in their frames. Suddenly the red Coast Guard helicopter zooms past, searchlights bright against the dusk. At the inlet they circle back, and I wonder if they intend to address the surfers, but no, evidently they regard them as hapless, self-endangering kooks, and leave them to their fate. The helicopter turns out to sea. Brave people. Almost dark, colors draining from the retina, the deepening storm extinguishing evening, salt water on coals. Mostly one watches the coconut palms, the pelicans nestled to the water, lights of neighboring condos coming on, penthouse giants dwarfing our sixty-year-old relic. Money is a force more powerful than the wind, humans more likely than hurricanes to wreak havoc upon us; this building will fall to the wrecking ball long before nature claims it.

SEPTEMBER 11

1.

Morning, stretching sore muscles on the floor by the bed,
sifting the night's quota of thoughts, images, tasks,
half-remembered insights, odd lines of poetry stranded

by the ebb and flow of the mind. So it is an ocean,
then, this Sea of Consciousness
mitigating, filtering, accommodating everything?

A child's unfinished alphabet puzzle on the sunporch
overlooking the reconfigured beach after the hurricane,
the beyond-dazzling shimmer of light across water.

Twenty-six letters, a to z, fingerable, adept.
Is it possible to intuit from these simplistic characters
Leaves of Grass, the *Duino Elegies*?

Who, shown a hydrogen molecule, would envision the sun?
As from leaf to rain forest, as from ant to biosphere,
as from a single brick to imagine Manhattan,

as from a human instant the totality of a life,
of lives interwoven, families and affiliations,
the time-trawled nets of societies and cultures.

So the arc of creativity is an ungrounded rainbow,
and cause for hope. Why distrust the universe?
We are engines burning violently toward the silence.

2.

Frigate birds in high wind over the inlet, enormous
    chains
of the construction cranes rattling like rusty wind chimes,
current running hard out through the channel,

schools of quick minnows along the rocks while midstream
the big fish wait for a meal, silver-gray flashes
of their torpedoing bodies—tarpon, bluefish, snook.

Heaps of seaweed on the beach, rim of clouds on the
    horizon
to mark the trailing edge of the storm pinwheeling
north to ravage the Carolinas, while along the jetty

Cuban fishermen with cruciform tattoos
are hand-netting baitfish to dump in old roofing buckets
like needling rain or schools of silver punctuation marks,

liquid semicolons seething in paratactic contortions,
prisoners seeking to deny a period to their sentence.
Surfers by the dozen—this is what they live for,

the cyclonic surge—waxing their boards,
paddling out, rising and tumbling.
Three fish on the sand, Jackson says they are cowfish,

one still breathing, we throw it back.
A few other families picking through the flotsam,
eelgrass, purplish crenellated whelks,

a brittle-shelled starfish,
his little polyp feelers probing our palms,
estrella de mar, estrellita,

butterflies lit by chimerical sunlight on orange-fingered
sea fern fronds, the smooth black coral trees
we use as Halloween decorations,

tubular mangrove seeds, coconuts and buoys,
blue and yellow tops of soda bottles,
pink cigarette lighters, a toothbrush, a headless doll.

3.

That they were called *towers*, the irony of that
ancient fortress word, twin strongholds, twin keeps,
that they fell and the day was consumed

in smoke of their ruination, in dust and ashen iota.
And the next day came and still the towers were fallen.
That morning I went for a long, aimless walk

along the beach, listening to *Blonde on Blonde*,
watching the sunlight stroke and calibrate the waves
like the silvery desire in Dylan's voice

as the skipped-heartbeat cymbals declared closure.
Later I met the gods emerging from a topaz-faceted sea,
their long hair flashing in the wind,

and the gods were beautiful, bold, and young,
and one called out to me as they arose and came forth.
Come and see the world we have created

from your suffering. And I beheld a city
where blood ran through streets the color of raw liver,
stench of offal and kerosene and torched flesh,

tongueless heads impaled on poles and severed limbs
strung on barbed wire beneath unresting surveillance
     cameras,
industrial elevators shuttling bodies to the furnace rooms,

and speakers blaring incongruous slogans, the tinkle of a
     toy piano,
maudlin and inane, and vast movie screens depicting
the glittering eyeballs of iron-masked giants,

and beyond the city hills of thorn trees and people in
     shanties
talking softly, awaiting their time in the carnage below.
No, no, laughed the god. *That is your world,*

the world we created is here—.
And I saw rolling hills carpeted in wildflowers,
tall grasses swaying in the wind,

no trees, no streams,
just grass and wind and endless light.
These fields are watered with human tears.

4.

Images of the aftermath: smoke and rubble,
gothic spire of a wall still standing, ash-white paper
blizzards of notary calculation like the clay tablets

of the Sumerians smashed and abandoned.
They seem, now, already, distant and historicized,
like Matthew Brady's Civil War photographs—

the dead sniper at Little Round Top, the Devil's Den,
blasted fields and ravaged orchards of the homeland.
And the camps of the Union Army,

numberless crates of supplies at the quartermaster's depot,
acres of wagon teams like the truckers
hauling debris away from Ground Zero, how Whitman

would have lauded their patriotic industry,
carting the wreckage of empire,
as he praised the young soldiers in their valor,

"genuine of the soil, of darlings and true heirs,"
as he cared for them in the army hospitals in Washington,
bringing to the wounded small, homely comforts—

apples, tobacco, newspapers, string,
pickles and licorice and horehound candy,
pocket change to buy a drink from the dairywoman

peddling fresh milk cot to cot in the field wards,
a comb, a book, a bowl of rice pudding
for Henry Boardman of the 27th Connecticut—

the democratic simplicity of his compassion,
whatever the erotic charge of its currency,
whatever its voyeuristic aspect,

discovering in the moment of material attention
the salve for a wounded life, and in the lives of the
    wounded
a serum for the injured nation. Meaning, by *compassion*,

his unique, coercive, actively embodied brand of
    empathy,
his conspiratorial love of self and other
intermingled, undivided, prelapsarian and entire,

his kindness, his tenderness,
Walt Whitman's tenderness is everything,
source of his greatness and key to his enigmatic soul,

the agent that calls sentimental platitudes to task
and elevates his grief into lasting eloquence,
the force that disavows anger for love

even amid the inconceivable
carnage of that war, the suffering of those men,
the magnitude of that national trauma.

But *Leaves of Grass* does not negate Gettysburg,
lilacs could not return Lincoln
to a grieving people,

no poem can refute the killing fields,
art will not stop the death squads
sharpening their machetes in the village square before
    dawn,

the militiamen, the partisans, the cutters-off of hands,
boy soldiers in new barracks throwing dice,
the child nailed to the hawthorn tree and the parents

beyond the barbed wire forced to admire the work of the
    nailers,
the nails themselves, iron ore and machines to quarry it,
mills and factories, depots and warehouses,

the distribution software,
the brown truck and the deliveryman,
wheelbarrows of lopped hands burned in pits with gasoline,

pretty smiling girls favored by the rape brigades,
the believers, the zealots, sergeants at arms, gangsters,
ethnic cleansers and counterinsurgency units,

tyrants, ideologues, defenders of justice,
technological sentinels in hardened bunkers
scanning infrared monitors for ignition signatures,

mass graves and secret facilities,
scientists chained to the lightning of matter,
the atoms themselves,

neutrinos and quarks, leptons
refracting alpha particles as words reflect
the stolen light of truth or revelation,

the faces of the terrorists as the airplane strikes the tower,
the faces of the firemen ascending the stairwell,
the faces of Stephen Biko's torturers at the amnesty
     hearing

while the dutiful son listens impassively
as if attending Miltonic lectures on human suffering,
the real, the actual, the earthly, ether of bodily want,

love and its granules pouring from the crucible,
rain to bathe the ingots, a gray horizon of muddy shoals
where oceangoing freighters are taken to pieces

by half-naked laborers wielding hammers and
    blowtorches,
a wrecking ground reverberating with gong-sounds
and the screams of yielding metal,

black-and-white photographs to document
that place, that labor, human history,
the work of men.

5.

Strange that we are born entire, red-faced and marsupial,
helpless but whole, no chrysalis or transformation
to enlarge or renew us, unless—who is to say that death

might not signify a wing-engendering reanimation
such as believers in the afterlife propose?
Is it a dream, then, this beach of seraphic sunlight,

silos full of clouds, monarch butterflies
flown from Mexico to roost on storm-uprooted trees
as schools of stingrays weave their way

through a realm of water which is their own,
the breaking through, the crossing over,
wingtips in the wave-curl

impinging upon us as ghosts or angels might,
cracks in the crystal spheres through which perfume
floods unending into our world?

Which passes, as lightning or a waning moon
drawn above the Atlantic, my Atlantic,
rose petals poured from silver goblets into molten glass,

nectar of apples and papayas,
shoes composed of wampum and desire,
my own Atlantic—but, why are you laughing?

Not at you, no.
Then with me?
No . . .

Clouds more enormous than souls,
more sacred, fatal, devoted,
saints climbing pearl-inlaid stairs into the burning sky,

saints or golden ants, but no—. *No?*
Are you sure? And the god smiled,
and picked up his scythe.

6.

Odor on the breeze of sea foam and decay,
the stars' genuflections,
subsidence, forgetfulness, the tides.

And beneath the still surface,
what depths?
And the creatures in the chasms below the waves?

All night I dreamed of mermaids caught in fishing nets
and now, jeweled with sargassum in the surf,
the body of a mermaid, drowned.

ORDER AND DISORDER

Long swim today: patterns of the sand on the ocean floor,
barely a wave, just the calm parallel sand ripples endlessly
repeated. And the places where

the pattern shifts, the sequence breaks

and then resumes on a different tangent or defile. Some-
thing white catches my eye, delta-shaped, a ray? Swim-
ming back, I clear my goggles to look: yes, it is a sting-
ray, dead, belly-up, gouged and eaten by a half-dozen
crabs, big crabs for hereabouts. Later I find three smooth
slabs from conch shells, an inch thick—must have been
monster conchs. I used to swim straight down the shore
here, a mile or more if the current was helping, but now
they've built a set of breakwaters and sandy coves to keep
the hard-won beach from eroding altogether, and this is
where the waves abandon what they tire of carrying. To-
day, hundreds of disk-shaped pieces of coral, chits or tiles
etched with floral geometries, like Paleolithic runes on a
Celtic passage tomb. Must have been groves of coral out
there, entire forests laid low by the hurricane's bulldozer.
So I quit swimming to gather it, fill hands and pockets,
and walk back along the beach.

What I value in the coral, its motifs and structures, its elegant engineering, what I perceive as beautiful is entirely incidental, calcified skeletal residue of the polyps' briefly efflorescing lives.

The hurricane, too, is beautiful, graven vortex swirled like the hair on an infant's skull,

blank eye of sharks and serial killers,

thermal engine driven across the equatorial Atlantic to incise a design of transformation upon us, mobile homes become driftwood, coral heads become stone coins.

Out of formlessness, order.

Against the darkness of the void, bright figures.

Have lived here twelve years now: one full year of the paradise of March, one full year of the anguish of September. April is not the cruelest month in Miami, April is not even close. Continue in this vein and one can deconstruct the canon of English literature in moments. Not deconstruct but dismantle, contradict, allow to decompose, like bean flowers on the compost heap.

———

Listening to the sound of the rain last night I thought: at least the plants are happy.

But how much rain can we endure before we rot?

———

Storm coming over the bay on the way to work, high winds churning violent charcoal clouds, and from the university, looking back, a swath of illumination frosted with sheets of lucent rain moving like dervishes across the green water, kinetic, serpentine, scriptural.

———

April is a pathetic fallacy.
April is a joke.

Patterns and schedules, forms and keys, life returning to normal: the boys at school and homework for me, teaching the graduate workshop until 8 o'clock tonight. Quick swim with Elizabeth, then we shower outside. Surely this is one of life's little-noticed pleasures, showering in dappled sunshine beneath a cerulean sky after a month-long siege of hurricanes. This shower was a masterstroke; it was, Elizabeth says, our greatest creation after only the children. Uprooting the ming aralias stout as knobby trees, erecting the fence, running the pipes across, laying down paving stones, sacks of smooth pebbles, lining it all with cheap rolls of bamboo fencing, like something Po Chü-i might have nailed together while waiting for the Emperor to recall him from exile. I mean, if Po Chü-i had shopped at Home Depot. Tell me, old master, how shall I express my gratitude for the good fortune of this life?

LUXURY

NOTEBOOK

LUXURY

Word-skeins,
ropes of language, flaxen cordage,
what luxury to coil its supple circumference

in spools, rolls, bobbins, reels,
weaving and looping, knotting, untangling,
slipping a blade to its fibers—

instead of history this entitlement,
this private wonder,
this poem.

ECLOGUE

1.

When Hiroshige turns the frame vertical
throughout *One Hundred Famous Views of Edo*,
his last great sequence of wood-block prints,
it is perhaps a nod toward photography—
he had seen some early examples,
tip of the western technological dagger—
though it also suggests a window, and so
makes the viewer complicit. And then
he deepens that dialogue by obscuring
or complicating the depicted landscape
with unusual angles of perspective
and wry compositional permutations:
there is a cinematic sense of depth
and motion to the images, varied as they are,
and the frame enters into the composition
as the delineating horizon of a door,
a pleasure boat, a temple or palanquin,
with, sometimes, an implied observer
having just left the scene—ink brush
set down hastily, blue robe on the floor,
a single hairpin removed from its pouch
in the courtesan's chamber. Sometimes
that observer is present at the margins
as an elbow or a shadow, as a horse, a cat,

wind-blown cuckoos. In my favorite
a turtle, bound and trussed and hung
from a cord, cranes its neck to look out
from the Mannen Bridge across meadows
and salt marshes full of fishermen
and white-sailed boats toward the distant city
and Mount Fuji on the far horizon.
I had assumed, studying it, that this turtle
had been trapped for sale as a food item—
the Japanese must like turtle soup?—
but have since discovered something
entirely marvelous: captive turtles
were sold to travelers not to be eaten,
but to be released back into the marsh,
as karmic offerings. . . .

2.

Taken away from Hiroshige by the doorbell:
a guy wanting to cut down my coconuts
and cart them away for *coco frio*.
Throughout Miami you can buy a cold coconut
to drink from the shell for a buck or two,
and this is my contribution to the local trade.
This man has a withered left hand—

the dexterity of cutting and catching
the coconuts as they fall already impressive,
how much more so with his disability.
In Miami Spanglish he calls me *boss*,
and I say, *Hay un otra árbol más grande atrás*,
my Spanish even worse than his poor English,
showing him the giant tree laden with dozens
of fat coconuts in the backyard, and he says
¡cocos tremendos! vowing to come back tomorrow
with a bigger ladder. I wonder if he will.
The same guys do not always return, season
after season, despite my eagerness to donate.
Only the newest arrivals work this job,
fresh from Cuba, Haiti, Colombia, Honduras,
and with luck a year is enough to climb a rung
upon that larger, metaphorical ladder.
These interactions with the *coco frio* guys
are always a highlight of my year. Why?
I suppose the sociological aspect is part of it,
grassroots American dreaming—but also
I have planted these coconut palms myself,
planted them as fishtailed shoots just sprouted
from the husk and now they are enormous
trees cascading coconuts across the yard,

so sending forth this crop, however humble,
is as close as I will ever get to being a farmer.
This is my pastoral. If I were Horace,
this would be an Ode. I mean Neruda. I mean,
if I were Virgil this would be an eclogue.

OCTOBER 7

1.

Sponges! The beach for three blocks covered with chunks and blobs of them, conical net-woven baskets and odd polymorphous hand shapes, like the giant foam fingers sold at sporting events, like that for an arena full of twisted aquatic gnomes. A little coral tossed up, some seaweed, but mostly the remains of what must have been a huge sponge bed, a sponge Atlantis. Why?

2.

Sponges all over the front porch, Elizabeth and Jackson busily spraying them with Lysol, soaking them in laundry buckets of bleached water like demoniacal bird's-nest soup. I tell them this will never work, we lack the subtle knowledge of the sponge makers, but who listens to me.

3.

Like strange mushrooms now, beneath the hibiscus bushes, the cast-off sponges, abandoned to the dirt.

The man is working with welding torch and grease gun on an old Florida East Coast Rail Road locomotive, alone in the sun with his chatty green parrot in a big field of weeds and fire ants and concrete rubble from which the last enduring shreds of hope for shade or succor have been splintered into stumps by Hurricane Andrew. Before the storm it was a railroad museum, rows of pines and palms and arching, cantilevered steel-beam train sheds; afterward a pile of twisted metal and tree trunks, tracks shunting rust as the grass prepares its final offensive. Long ago it was a zeppelin hangar at the old Naval Air Station, but not even a party of seven-year-olds playing whistle tag can wake the ghosts of the airship pilots or Flagler's engineers.

Is this the locomotive from 1913?

The man lays his torch on the gravel, rags the grease from a faded hula-girl tattoo, and says 1924. Last of its kind. 1924 the F.E.C. bought twenty of these, run 'em awhile, sold three up to the Arkansas–Gulf Coast Rail Road in 1930. They run 'em awhile, then took their best engine and best tender and run those together all the way up to 1957, where they had some tracks used to flood about three feet of water, you couldn't run any electric locomotive through there. Had it in a park in Texarkana forty years just falling apart before we brought it back here where it started.

Does it still run?

Will when we get through fixing it. Maybe two years. Gonna run it down to Homestead on the old F.E.C. right-of-way. Got new flues, new bearings, working now to get the sheet metal off the boiler, climb in there in our space suits, clear all the asbestos out—one thing about asbestos, you can chew on it, you can eat it, just don't breathe it into your lungs. Aiming for the Fourth of July, take it up to Fort Lauderdale full of steam, run it all the way to Jacksonville, maybe.

Maybe, says the wind or an echo.

a-b   a-b   a-b

Hey, what's the parrot's name?

The man says Archimedes and the parrot cries Eureka and the engine whispers I think I can and the wind says give me a place to stand and I will move the world.

1.

Here is a view of the cloth-dyers' stalls in Konda Street
with *Fujisan* white in the distance and a sky
alive with small birds, wrens and larks,
flags and streamers and paper carp rustling in the wind
above the city, prosperous, blossoming, early spring.

Here is a view of the timberyards in the Fukagawa district,
two men poling lashed rafts of logs against the shore,
rooftops cloaked in snow, trees illuminated with it,
small dogs, an umbrella, two sparrows
and snowflakes above the deep blue Sumida River.

Here is a view of the Ryōgoku Bridge, crowds sheltering
in teahouses from a summer storm, wide water
full of ferries, work vessels delivering rice, silhouette
of a courtesan against the drawn blinds of a pleasure boat
amid mimosa blossoms, early evening, plum rain.

Three views of the city: that is enough for one day.

2.

Soji, the block-cutter, makes merry with the woodsmen
who bring the choicest logs from the mountains,

pouring hot sake in his workshop against an autumn chill
with rustic fellows for whom Edo, in its complexity,
must resemble a bouquet of chrysanthemums and thorns.

In this way, filial, plied with rice wine, lovers
of the same forest goddess,
the finest wood is obtained at small cost.

Yamakazura, wood of the wild cherry tree.

Only heartwood will suffice for the master line block,
softer wood for the color blocks, cut from the same tree,
patiently, so they will shrink at the same rate.

Paper makers, printers, ink-pigment grinders,
forgers of awls and fine chisels,
my brush is my own to paint with as I will
but the art of reproduction relies upon many craftsmen.

Why fear technology? Why fear the West?

The Americans in their black ships bring
marvels of ingenuity but nothing I cannot imagine
my own hands creating in time.

At first, it is true, their photographs possessed
the magical articulation of a talking bird,
but already I have gleaned their insights,
placing the gnarled limb of the Sleeping Dragon Plum Tree
hard in the foreground, branches growing beyond
the horizon of a frame neither rigid nor sacrosanct.

Reflections on water, the sun behind a cloud,
their light effects appear contrived, lacking in subtlety,
yet a bright moon does cast shadows,
and this may be illustrative of winter nights,
streets of the Yoshiwara thronged with revelers.

Why fear a shadow? Why fear the frame?

Frames are a convention of art's limitation.
They remind pictures of their mortality
as moon shadows prove that I am human and corrupt.

3.

Waking from a dream: the city is burning
and I am the fire warden.
It is my inheritance, my jurisdiction and duty.

Still I can do nothing but stare from the watchtower
as the cloth-dyers' banners flare into fiery ribbons
and the lumberyards curl with orange flame.

In the morning I am taken by the Shogun's magistrates
and led through the streets in disgrace.

The fire began here, they say, coming to a place
I recognize as the workshop of the carver, Soji.
It is full of cherrywood blocks, master templates
of all my prints, thousands upon thousands.

These, they say, were the first to burn.

I'm still slogging Sam's surfboard across the sand when the boys race off to see what the commotion up the beach is all about, and by the time I get close they've run back to report, a sea turtle, a leatherback, the biggest of them all, we've never seen one before, but there's a problem, it's injured, they've already loaded it into the back of the Fish & Game Department pickup truck as the local cops pointlessly holler to stand back, stand back, and it is truly huge, like an old sequoia log, like the barnacled hull of an overturned rowboat, one of the rangers says it is probably eighty years old, and the boys say its fins are all chopped up by a boat, but the ranger says no, a knife, and now I can see sinewy stumps where the flippers should be, gray flesh marbled with milk-white fluid, sickening, I turn away, it must have washed here from some place where turtles are still a food source, the Bahamas are less than a hundred miles east, there's a strong wind blowing Portuguese men-of-war up on the beach, sea turtles eat jellyfish, the tentacles blind them as they age, these waves have brought us all here today, some surfers already out, others in the crowd talking about the turtle, I'm turning to head back when I see the bad look on Elizabeth's face, some of the white-haired retirees from the next building are telling her the full story, it crawled from the ocean at dawn, it didn't lay eggs, it didn't swim away, they thought it was old, maybe sick, they called the police, the fishermen from the jetty wandered over to look, one man rode it like a horse, before it's clear what's happened, or why, a fishing knife emerges to saw through the rubbery, elephant-thick skin, three flippers gone before anyone stops him, the senior citizens are shouting out, hey, no! accosting him, what are you doing? why did you do this? and he: *for soup*, some of the old people are crying, they chase him away, get lost! you're crazy, how would you feel if we cut your arm off like that? some of the fishermen laughed, some shook their heads, the police arriving helpless, uninformed, it's more than I can handle, honestly, I turn away, I am trembling not with anger but with shame, the ranger truck spins its wheels and bogs down in soft sand having traveled perhaps fifty feet, it takes an hour before a tractor comes to tow them clear, the giant turtle is that heavy, what is there to say? eighty years old, for soup, that milky extrusion— was it blood? as I dive into the water I am thinking how generous the ocean is in its forgiveness, I am thinking at least I never looked into its eyes.

Ovarian cysts are not at all uncommon, and they are likely to be benign. They often can be suppressed hormonally, and that's why we had you on the birth control pills a couple years ago—and they did resolve, then, which is why they disappeared from the ultrasounds. Unfortunately, they've come back, bilaterally, which accounts for the discomfort you've been experiencing. And on this side, there is an area, uh, a *spot* that concerns me a little bit—you can see it here, on the left. Could be many things—tissue, hair or teeth, sometimes those cells cling to the walls of the uterus and develop and become encysted. Normally we would perform a biopsy, but given your pain level right now, and the persistence of the cyst, I want to schedule surgery. To remove both cysts, biopsy anything we find—of course, we don't know precisely what we'll find until we get in there—but in all likelihood we will be able to preserve both ovaries, or at least the right one, and the uterus. But I will need you to sign consent forms for their removal, should that procedure be necessary. I think we should attend to this right away, as soon as we can schedule the surgery. Next week, or the week after. Any questions?

THE TOAD

In the courtyard of our house there is a fountain
in the form of a whitewashed dolphin
leaping from a scalloped, algae-ridden bowl
in which a rag-eared antler of stag coral sits bleaching.

The sun here is fierce enough to burn away the water
in three or four days, and this morning
I am tasked to fill it again, and to clear the small pump
of fallen leaves and alamanda blossoms,

feeling weary, hollowed out, frayed and startled
enough to drop the watering can with a jolt
at the tingling signal of an animal presence,
the sudden awareness of another living creature at hand,

that sensory aura or electrical field felt
and recognized by some nerve-kernel of the brain
undiscarded through all our baroque evolution.
It is a toad. Big as my fist, cloud-gray,

its rubbery head emerging from the fountain's murk
like a weird, grinning, operatic goblin mask.
When it blinks the camera lenses of its uncanny eyes
I can see that they are gold, brilliant and metallic,

like moon-lander foil hammered over robotic orbs.
My heart is pounding like a piston,
like the fine hammer of that goldsmith. It aches
profoundly as a torn bicep. All week I have been lashed

and scoured by an ocean of phantoms
and I am worn smooth as beach glass,
deeply exhausted, and more than a little bit lost.

Faster and faster our children are disappearing
into the mist of the future
even as we shout into our parents' ears
to remind them of the past. Do you remember it,

father? Do you?

More than ever I lean upon Elizabeth,
like the clothes of a scarecrow upon its staff.

My cloak to ward the rain from her skin.
My hat to fend the sun from her brow.
My crooked smile to scatter the grackles.

Do you remember, father?
Do you remember any of it—

the steep slate roof on which the trees
rained down their hoard of summer acorns—

a green station wagon skating an exit ramp
into the icy meadow of a cloverleaf
in slow motion, unstoppable, unharmed—

a picnic by a ruined mill
where three mountain streams converged—

where was that place, can you tell me,
do you remember?

Yes, I remember—it was long ago, in Italy.

You were a child and I carried you up the mountain
and you swam with your brother in the pools
of melted snow run down from the Alps to the millpond
past dark hill towns like the dwellings of trolls,
older than the Romans, much older,
and I swam beside you in the ice-green water,
and rested on hot boulders in the sunshine,
the muscles of my back grew warm as the ropes of a sailboat,

I was strong, your mother was beautiful,
we ate bread and cheese where a fig tree
burdened the soil with its wild, discarded seeds,
we walked up the stream, collecting stones,
floating sticks over tiny cataracts,
we startled a toad from a rock and watched it
struggle to swim away, paddling its elastic arms
and bowing its webbed legs against the current
to hold its place exactly,
neither moving forward nor slipping back,
a strange, knobbed, ancient creature,
like the unlucky prince transformed by an ogre,
like the king of the mountain in disguise,
and when we rescued him, exhausted, to the grassy bank,
what was it he whispered to me alone?

I am neither prince nor troll
nor toad
but time itself.

Every instant of your existence
belongs to me
but I give you this moment as my gift.

Remember this day, this hour, this very second.
Guard it well.
Keep it as I would keep it.

For when next you see me
know that I have come to reclaim
what you have failed to treasure sufficiently.

Know that my realm is eternal and inhuman.
Know that I am merciless.
Know me by my golden eyes.

What do you think about there, in that room of fawn and putty wallpaper, blond wood and green floral up-holstery, in the Women's Oncology Center, looking up at the pepper-spackled ceiling tiles, waiting? Do you think, what are the odds? Do you think, we shall persevere, we shall not be deterred? Do you think, we were lucky to get a space so close to Ambulatory Surgery, and the moon above the parking lot in the predawn sky aligned with a single star and fat Venus shining, two good omens? Do you think how much this resembles the morning eight years ago to the month when Jackson was born, or, wait, how many years? Do you think, looking at those around you, that they resemble refugees lined up for soup or Red Cross blankets, that they suggest bundled bodies at the door of some Soviet ministry to beg information, the location of a son, the cause of a wife's disappearance? But what was her crime, Commissar, what was her crime? And still they disappeared, year after year, by the thousands and the millions, into Stalin's unfathomable slaughterhouse. To promulgate death! To surrender to it as we surrender to the bright machinery of hope, the ring of invisible rays that will reveal our fate, the instruments and stoppered vials, latex gloves, floors being mopped and in need of mopping, the nurses' station with its teddy bears and be-ribboned photographs of high school graduations, doctors gliding silkily past, attendants to the mystery, acolytes gowned in caustic white and surgical green? Do you think, with a smirk, how much this resembles the waiting room at the Toyota dealer as they clean the carbon buildup from the fuel injector system, all the valve jobs and tune-ups to slow the engine's inevitable decline? Do you think how much the worn linoleum reminds you of the North Dade Justice Center, crowds arrayed to receive their fateful dispensation from blunt, impersonal representatives of the system, young women battling obesity lined up for new driver's licenses, young men straggling into traffic court in flip-flops and torn camouflage pants, in gold chains and Snoop Dogg T-shirts, old women dozing in the corners, middle-aged men in service uniforms—janitors, security guards, parking attendants—filling out forms in a version of the language they will never master, a smiling family attired in matching soccer jerseys from the Selección Nacional de Honduras waiting for which adjudication to be handed down, which fateful dispensation? Do you feel how powerful a force compassion is, and that to open its floodgates here would be to risk inundation? Do you think, studying the amoeba-shaped plaster patches and water stains on the walls, that the mind resembles an amoeba, pulsing and probing, negotiating obstacles, searching out nutrients? Do you think that the earth is a waiting room from which we shall depart only when summoned by death? *They are ready for you now, Mr. McGrath, please go in.* Do you think, secretly, in the inmost chamber of your being, take them all and spare mine? Take them all into your black dominion, Commissar, even the healthy ones, if so you require, even the visitors reading magazines and the sour-faced children, the fear-stricken mothers and the husbands watching TV—take them all and leave for another day those I love—take even from mine in fair measure if you must, take the ovaries for they have been duly productive, take the uterus for it may be honorably relinquished, take a kidney if it so pleases you, take from the liver that it may regenerate, take, take, take, leaving only what cannot be spared. Do you think, even the second time the hand grasps your shoulder, that it must be an echo or self-inquisition when that voice begins to speak? *The doctor would like to see you. Please come with me.* And another voice, like a fiery blazon, saying *The surgery went well. Pathology indicates all the tissue is benign. Your wife is going to be just fine.*

That sound is the thrashing of paper lanterns against the
    eaves.
Vessels frail as bodies lit with incandescent blood,
what else but that to survive the storm? What else could
    there be
to hold back the darkening rain of the city, empathy
like an opal, sorrow like a shriveled raisin
in the dust beneath the stove
but still a raisin. Pockets of odd coins, lint
to speak for transience and the rusted metal of fallen
    leaves,
paper cups with pastel scrimshaw elephants or diamonds,
    whatever
yolk the dawn subscribes for our delectation,
whatever throne the night sees fit to claim from the angels.
Difficult, difficult. All of it, any of it—
schoolgirls, vendors of sunglasses, businessmen
trembling their woes toward destiny and sleep—to feel it
or perish in the wicks of unlit candles,
to begin again within the inked shells of Easter eggs.
Steam is rising from grates, a child
pedals a bicycle through the alleyway of ghosts unafraid.
Purity, the maw of it, blackbirds and kestrels
against a sky the color of antique mah-jongg tiles, color of
    aspirin

dissolving in seawater as the sun bursts its amnion
of tattered clouds like the raw carcass of the heart
    revealed.
That sound is the ticking of paper lanterns in the storm.
Just that. It is hard
in the radiance of this world to live
but we live.

ASTRAL

NOTEBOOK

THE INDIVISIBLES

They exist: atoms,
components, letters, vertebrae.
It exists: the totality of it,
historical spine, the universal
discourse of space
composed of numerals
causal and oblique as berry pickers
scouring the thickets of the mind
which is the wind and so
windmills to crush the berries
and flavor the wonderful
bread with jam at breakfast.
Sun up, the world begins,
and it is composed
of energy and matter
like pigs in blankets or eggs
in cartons despite the odds.
Cities rise to face the dawn,
lathes, potter's wheels, smoke
from the censers of hilltop temples,
the mind chasing a wagon of illumination
through the mechanical universe,
dutiful dog, eager and oblivious
as the worm in time's apple

or the kid telling jokes
in the planetarium
the instant after the lights go out
and before the stars turn on.

MIDDLE AGE

Like Hiroshige's boatmen guiding their raft
down a widening river
past banks overburdened with cherry blossoms

we approach middle age
and begin
to drift away from things,

beliefs, ideals, ideas,
people calling out from shore—*hello!*
Star-throated flowers, the lucid

haven of the current.
Good-bye, old friends,
good-bye.

THEN

What happens then, after the stars explode, after the
    universe expands to the limits of possibility,
after the bones of the last animals disappear into the
    plains, and melt into the dirt, and rise up as corn,
rise up as grass blowing in the autumn winds that carry
    the soil back to the sea as the oceans boil away
and the galaxies recoil into swirling matter, and the
    earth becomes a single ripple, a single integer in that
    equation?

What happens then, how does the story turn out, the
    social narratives in many languages, the striving
    cultures,
new definitions of justice, new plans for a rebuilt city,
    leaders and followers, a championship season,
plots and dramas we each have played our small part in,
    our domestic sentence, our phrase or motif,
our single character— *&* or *q*—whichever shape our
    being has pressed into the ledger of time?

What happens after our works have all been forgotten,
    the paintings lost, the architecture collapsed,
when the last books have fallen into the sea to be
    consumed by whales, digested by shrimp and minnows,

when our music no longer echoes, and lampreys alone
   read the poetry of humanity in the dim library of the
   deep?

What happens after the body fails, after the noise of the
   blood falls still, the lungs grow stiff,
after the white bird ascends from the marsh at dawn to
   escort the soul to the borders of this realm,
the day, the hour, the moment after—what happens then,
   what happens then?

Surges and lulls, work and family, almost a month since my last notebook entry: if I didn't write it down, did it really happen? The year is vanishing; time floods past; it burns us, it heals us, irradiating every cell in our bodies, like starlight. Sometimes I think I can see it moving, the little seconds hopping like fleas, the hours racing away, finger sandwiches devoured by wild dogs. How little a year means—but not nothing; the earth does orbit the sun, tulips do await the spring. Sometimes I read aloud all the poems Sylvia Plath wrote in 1963, to feel the power life exerted upon her even as she slid toward its extinction. Sometimes I listen to all the songs John Lennon recorded in 1966, music he dreamed out of the great boiling loneliness of his twenties, like wax melting from the comb and foxglove of his organs, fame destroying him slowly, like tuberculosis, but not yet, not yet.

Years, says the cosmos—what do I care about years?

I own no instrument calibrated finely enough to detect their passage.

My calculus lacks the zeros to enumerate their throng.

But why should we indulge the cosmos' delusions of grandeur, why engage its gaudy ego, why even listen when we can live?

————

On February 21, 1888, Van Gogh leaves Paris for Arles, arriving, against all odds, not in the warm, color-saturated south he had sought, but a desolate Provence buried beneath two feet of snow—"like the winter landscapes of the Japanese," he writes to Theo. He works indoors, painting shoes, potatoes, a basket of oranges, a sprig of blossoming almond branch in a jar. Soon the orchards are in full bloom, apricot and peach and cherry, and later fields of grain, ten paintings of wheat fields in the last week of June alone—"I am in a perpetual fever of work," he writes— the daily task, the hourly urgency to create, draw and redraw, paint and copy and move to the next orchard, the next meadow or subject, fishing boats on a sea of reed pen sussurations, farmers walking down the road, stars above the Rhone, the night café, barges and washerwomen, self-portraits, portraits of the Zouave, of Madame Ginoux, oleanders, sheaves of grain, the yellow house. Next canvas, and the next. Lovers in the park, flower beds, haycarts, portraits of the Roulins' bulb-headed infant, the sunflowers he paints to welcome Gauguin, the sower, the reaper, the garden of the poet. From the day of his arrival until December 23, when he cuts off his ear, when his collapse begins, he creates a total of 298 paintings and drawings. And then, in his final decline, through eighteen months of illness and institutionalization, as if he might paint his way back toward health and sanity, another 470 works.

Neruda, to commemorate his seventieth birthday, intended to publish, as a gift to his readers, seven new volumes of poetry—seven!—but he died nine months too soon, Chile in flames around him, Santiago echoing with the Generalissimo's jackboots.

Yes, but the work was done, the poems were written, the books were published posthumously, in Argentina.

All year the walls of my office have been papered with sets of images that move me deeply, prints on magnet boards, postcards from friends, pages torn from art books taped above the desk, mainly the works of Hiroshige and Van Gogh, and now, just as Neruda has been returned to the bookshelves, I am wondering what to install in their place:

Cornell boxes, Hopper paintings, maps of ancient cities, comic book covers;

black-and-white photographs of atom bomb tests from the 1950s—"Easy," "Diablo," "Yellowwood," "Stokes";

Maoist propaganda posters and the figures of La Lotería;

images of apocalypse and of paradise from Hieronymus Bosch to *The Fabulous Region of Himavant*, a realm of multicolored elephants and lotos-eating deities taken from a nineteenth-century Burmese cosmology;

deep-space images of galaxies and nebulae, great swirls of light and color which are not so different, after all, from *The Starry Night*.

———

Vincent first conceives *The Starry Night* that April in Arles, when the orchards resemble euphoric star fountains; he has been reading Walt Whitman—"Song of Myself" had just been translated into French, selections of *From Noon to Starry Night*—and he writes to Theo: "I also must have a starry night with cypresses, or perhaps surmounting a field of ripe corn." "I want to make some drawings in the manner of Japanese prints," he writes. "I can only go on striking as long as the iron is hot." One year earlier, in Paris, he spent countless hours poring through Japanese woodblocks at Samuel Bing's famous gallery, working to master their language of slashes and crosshatchings, gouges and swirls, and copied in oil paint two of Hiroshige's *Hundred Famous Views of Edo*. He paints *The Starry Night* from the asylum at Saint-Rémy, in June of 1889, the same year Whitman publishes his valedictory *Collected Poems and Prose* before suffering a stroke that leaves him "cabin'd with illness," in Camden, for twenty months. Whitman dies in 1892, outliving Van Gogh by two years. The year of Van Gogh's birth, 1853, Whitman is working as a carpenter in Brooklyn, distilling his inchoate amative and vortical poetics toward their mysterious crystallization, just beginning the sustained writing that will yield the first edition of *Leaves of Grass* in 1855, the second edition the following year, 1856, which also sees the publication of the initial prints from *One Hundred Famous Views of Edo*. Even as Whitman guides the sheets of his galleys through the letterpress, walking daily to the Rome brothers' printing shop on the corner of Cranberry and Fulton, Hiroshige's drawings are pasted to ebony blocks of cherrywood, and carved by master carvers, and inked, and pressed deep into the paper by the burin at the publisher Uoya Eikichi's, revealing the grain of the wood like a testament of the forest spirit, or the ghost of Hiroshige himself, whose death, in the cholera epidemic of 1858, brings the series to its conclusion. If *The Starry Night* is Vincent's translation of Whitman's cosmological dynamism into surging graphic articulation it is also the realization of his mastery of compositional techniques acquired from Hiroshige. Thus it transpires that Whitman and Hiroshige, who of course knew nothing of each other's lives, or work, find their point of contact, their moment of artistic fusion, in the image-haunted mind of a red-haired Dutch painter roaming the corridors of an asylum in the south of France.

————

For Hiroshige art was a craft, for Van Gogh it was a
    ministry.

For Lennon death was an unimaginable accident, for
    Plath a visionary ambition.

For Whitman poetry was an ecstatic invocation to the
    universe of the self, for Neruda a declaration of the
    selfless universal.

At last, the preparations
for my Whitman and Neruda seminar
have begun!

THE WORK

Swimming today, caught and spun in the breakers at the
sandbar, flung and whirled underwater, pummeled in
that grasp I recognize, suddenly, that this is the same vis-
ceral energy Van Gogh seeks to capture not only in *The
Starry Night* but everywhere in the late work—mountains
and clouds burning with vigilance, olive trees frenzied
as Hiroshige's whirlpools—a frenzy which is neither his-
trionic nor hyperbolic but an attempt to depict the vital,
shimmering plasma of existence. Which may be impos-
sible. Like the lifeless sponges crumbled to dust beneath
a flowering hedge. Like the fish out of water, iridescent
star-rime draining from its eye, its brilliance fading back
to three-dimensionality—what is that lost dimension if
not time itself? How to reclaim it, portray it, or acknowl-
edge, at least, its absence, how to depict existence outside
of time, unfiltered, raw—like the feeling of encroaching
upon a state of timelessness that arrives, if you are lucky,
during the act of creation, working oneself to the edge of
the reaper's blade, prow of the icebreaker, the figurehead,
ruby-eyed stargazer glazed with sea foam, the relentlessly
forward-looking labor of art, its sense of momentum,
hurtling onward, almost capturing the smoke trail of
some immense and wondrous beast, a creature fleshed
with power—the work, the work—the work is diamonds
crushed to powder and atoms breaking their chains

215

and galaxies born in robes of red hydrogen—the past is everywhere in our roiled wake, fluorescent monocells fading back to ink-black night, and the present is a figment, a riddle of physics, pure gesture, stroke and glide—only the future is real and we can write our way toward it, paint our way into it, create a path, steel chisel from which the marble leaps in glinting slivers—riding the neck of the beast, catching up, crashing through the underbrush, reaching a hand toward the hem of its garment, reaching out—there, there—almost—craning forward—there—almost, almost. . . .

THE FUTURE

I would speak to it as to a stream in the forest
where infant ferns grow shapely as serpents or violins.

I would surrender to it if I could drift among the stars
as among a cloud of milkweed spores, or jellyfish.

Years turn, like autumn leaves; they pass,
and we number them, like galaxies or symphonies,
when we should honor them with names,
like hurricanes, or the craters of the moon.

What will Arcturus ever mean to me
compared to these years—1962, 1986, 2005?

They march beside me like siblings,
they are more intimate than lovers,
they do not turn back when I fall behind.

The future watches us and marvels
at our inability to comprehend it.

Even Einstein only glimpsed its shores,
like Magellan, planting small vineyards
at the edge of the ice, like Erik the Red.

To view it plainly we would need to evict
the self from its rough settlement,
to strip the bark from our limbs and branches,
to reside in a place where atoms and stars
resemble shy animals learning to eat from our hand.

Only then would the future, like a lonely hermit,
find its way to that clearing by the stream in the forest,
and sit beside us on a mossy stone, and listen.

STARS

They possess an aspect as of gravity, as of the void
to fill which our hearts offer themselves
upon altars of moonlight.

The vastness and tinyness of existence
is like a holy text writ upon a grain of rice, or a star.

The way attention skitters from light on wineglasses
table to table resembles them, as too
a bossa nova symphony of bassoons and slide guitar.

The loneliness of atoms is astonishing,
like the sight of stars from a vessel at sea.

The night retains textures and empathies
that might be signals from angels or distant stars,
and the trees assume dream-shapes
we do not recognize and can never truly know.

Stars are but diacritical marks
upon the night's cosmological syntax.

We are human, and our form is a corruption of starlight
poured like heavy syrup into soft-skinned molds,
like decorative soaps, or candles.

Like the stars we burn fiercely, reluctantly,
as a dragon consumes its golden hoard.

Of my eyes, of my skin, the stars shall know nothing.

DECEMBER 30

Driving home from Marco Island along the Tamiami Trail, out of the 10,000 Islands' bottomless salad bar, one-note symphony of the mangrove forest, Devonian green, and then the giraffe-colored grasslands of winter in South Florida, palmettos and sawgrass beneath a benevolent sky, devotional blue, then the nature boardwalk at Fakahatchee Strand, statuesque cypresses among the few uncut survivors, wild royal palm, mossy live oak, poplar oak,

and the swamp shrubs knee-deep in water,
pond apple and pop ash and wild coffee,
sword fern, alligator flag,

and we see:

buzzards perched on the lowest branches, ornery and
    grotesque
woodstork high up a dead limb
hurricane-damaged nest of the bald eagles repaired for
    new fledglings
some smaller birds, no positive ID
a raccoon scrubbing its front paws fastidiously in the muck
small alligators in repose among the water lilies
ten-foot alligator sunning on a log

"Well," says Jackson, "that's a big alligator."

Onward.

Crowded with German tourists no stop for lunch at
  Joanie's Blue Crab too bad.

Clyde Butcher's photo gallery festooned with holiday
  lights, mostly empty, the boys tossing rocks in the pond.

Almost home, approaching Miami, just beyond the sub-
urban perimeter we pull in to the Native American Arts
Festival at the Miccosukee reservation: blue-raspberry Sno-
Kones and pan-Amerindian handicrafts from Bolivian pan-
pipes to Navajo blankets, gimcrack bows and arrows, dry-
frond dolls in Seminole patchwork, and Johnny Cypress in
a Santa Claus hat wrestling alligators in a concrete tank,
the ancient manifestation of their diamond-black bodies,
imperious visitors from the Age of Reptiles—

three small girls kicking a purple ball in the gravel,

oily smell of fry bread, boiled corn,

at the bandstand a performance by Klingit dancers from
Alaska in dark mantles beaded with clan symbols, raven
and eagle and coho salmon, bear and orca and the love-
birds, *which is the eagle and the raven,* explains the regal,
delicate-voiced dance master, softly laughing in the click-
ing glottals and tongue-popping vocables of his native
speech,

because in the old days those clans had to marry each other,
but nowadays we marry whoever we want,
but the young ladies asked me not to say that
cuz they're getting too many proposals after the show!—

as I notice just beyond the stage's half-painted backdrop
the vast southern sweep of the grasslands commence, the
Everglades, immediate and grave and theatrical, like a set
of impossible dimension suspended in the wings,

and this next dance is a wedding dance,
and the song is a lovesong,
I can't teach it all to you, but the first line, in Klingit, goes:

the world has flooded over me.